"How are
making any un
"Of course ___, y ___
teasing in his tone and responded in like. "He's been a
perfect gentleman."

"Aye, I'd expect no less. Knowing his brother as I
do, I would believe the men of that family are
honorable."

"Reverend Wallace has a brother, here in this
community?"

"He does. Harry Wallace. Together with Brodie
MacMillan, he runs the largest milling operation in
nearly two hundred miles. He's married and has seven
stepchildren and a pair of twins of his own blood. Quite
the New World entrepreneur and gentleman."

"Are the brothers close?"

"I understand not. A dispute back in the Highlands
years ago separated them, and they've never made it
up."

"How sad." She stood. "I must be getting back. I
have a meal to prepare." She put a hand on Douglas's
broad shoulder before he could get up. "It's lovely to
have you close by. I hope my coming hasn't caused any
distress to your lovely wife."

"Dunnae greet, lass." Grinning, he lapsed into deep
Highland brogue as he stood. "I'll manage. I can be
right charmin' when I put my mind to it."

Praise for Gail MacMillan

HEATHER FOR A HIGHLANDER won three honors at the Trans Canada Romance Writers Maple Leaf Awards: Best Heroine, Second Favorite Hero, and Honorable Mention for the ending.

"I love, love, loved this book! It…begins with a murder, and ends with a fiery romance. And all because of a horse bet between brothers. I mean, isn't that how all good stories begin?"~*Romance Novels for the Beach*

"Read in one sitting, which hardly ever happens for me. Truly engaging. I would definitely pick up another book by this author." *~judge at TransCRW competition*

"Be prepared to be hooked on the first word of the first page [of *COWBOY COUNTRY CONFESSIONS*] and go on to the next with anticipation."
          ~Rebecca Melvin, Publisher, Double Edge Press

"Gail MacMillan's stories delight the senses and brighten the dark days of winter like a candle glowing on a windowsill."
          ~Sue Owens Wright, author, newspaper columnist

"I love this little adventure [*HOLDING OFF FOR A HERO*]!…surprises…one light, wonderful read."
          ~The Romance Reviews (4 Stars)

"Not sure who I like better, [the] German Shepherd, the Pug, or the sexy next door neighbor."
          ~Matilda, Coffee Time Romance & More (5 Cups)

"Not your typical romance story [*SHADOWS OF LOVE*], but I couldn't put it down."
          ~Michelle, Cocktails and Books (4 Cups)

Lottie's Legacy

by

Gail MacMillan

Riverhaven Rogues

Lottie's Legacy

Cover Art by *The Wild Rose Press, Inc.*

The Wild Rose Press, Inc.
PO Box 708
Adams Basin, NY 14410-0708
Visit us at www.thewildrosepress.com

Publishing History
First Edition, 2022
Trade Paperback ISBN 978-1-5092-4054-8
Digital ISBN 978-1-5092-4055-5

Riverhaven Rogues
Published in the United States of America

Dedication

In loving memory of Joey,
a little dog with a big heart

Chapter One

Barely conscious, bruised and bleeding, Lottie Danvers lay in the Edinburgh gutter and begged for death to end her misery. In the midnight darkness, a bitter March wind peppered her with rain, and ice pellets assaulted her.

The clop of horses' hooves on the stones of the street and the creak of wheels roused her. Were they returning?

Horror engulfed her. Frantic, she struggled to get to her feet. Failing, she slumped back into the filth and waited, heart pounding hard against her chest.

"Stop!" The command brooked no refusal.

Horses snorted and stamped. A door rasped open and booted footsteps strode toward her. They halted by her side.

"Good God!" a male voice muttered. Through half-opened eyes she saw a figure, water spouting from the brim of his hat, bending over her.

"No!" Terror wrenching at her heart, she held up a hand in the only protest she could muster as he dropped on one knee beside her.

"Don't be frightened." His tone was gentle. "I mean you no harm."

She tried to speak, but all that came from her lips was a broken moan. Defeated, she let her hand drop to her side.

"Biggs, hold the horses steady." Strong arms gathered her up. "We're to have a passenger."

In a dizzy haze of pain, too weak to protest, she was lifted into a carriage and placed on a padded seat.

"Drive on," a sharp command and a rap on the roof ordered.

As the vehicle lurched forward, the movement brought a gasp from her lips.

"Rest," the male voice soothed. "You're safe."

She tried to focus on her companion but saw only a male silhouette in the darkness. Lottie slumped into a corner as a dry garment was placed over her. The soft wool offered a measure of comfort, and she clutched at it.

I'm not going to die in the gutter was her last conscious thought.

****

"He that is without sin among you, let him first cast a stone at her."

Looking out over his meagre congregation, Reverend Jack Wallace ended his reading. A sixteen-year-old girl on the front bench and a white-haired, bearded gentleman on the one at the rear were his only audience.

The irony of the situation made a corner of Jack's mouth twitch. Apparently he'd chosen the text for his homily too late. His flock had already judged him and found his sin too grievous to forgive. He'd hoped in a university town like Fredericton, New Brunswick, in the spring of 1819, people would be sufficiently broadminded to accept him.

"Let us conclude this Sabbath's service with the singing of the hymn 'Amazing Grace.' " He drew a deep breath and plunged ahead.

Raising his voice in the familiar words, he began. The girl stood, shoulders back, head held high, and joined him. The elderly man at the rear clutched his cane and struggled to his feet to add his support in a deep, resonating baritone.

When they ended the hymn, Jack raised his hands and offered a benediction, "May the Good Lord bless and keep you."

He closed his eyes for a moment. Then he descended from the pulpit and walked down the center aisle to the door. The girl followed, hands clasped, head bowed, the man wearing spectacles behind her. When the trio moved outside onto the church's top step into the foggy drizzle of a bleak March morning, Jack saw a collection of a dozen young men across the street. Standing amid patches of melting snow, they glared at him.

"A fine homily, John." Above his snowy beard, the man from the rear bench smiled at him through thick spectacles. "Most fitting."

"Thank you, Theodore." With a rueful grin, he shook the man's proffered hand. "I had prayed for a wider audience."

"Your flock, as you so often generously call them, are a collection of judgmental fools!" The man's voice rose with indignation. "What you've done in no way..."

A clod of earth stuck the church door beside them.

"Heathen!" The word rang out from among the group in the street. Another lump hit the building. "Sinner!"

"Excuse us, Professor, but I think we'd best be going." Jack took his daughter's arm. "Come along,

3

Cathy."

"Yes, yes, I quite agree." The elderly man gripped his cane with a vehemence that whitened his knuckles. "If I were younger…"

"If you were younger, Theodore, what I can guess you'd be contemplating wouldn't be a wise move."

"I suppose you're right." The professor sighed. "You'll have to forgive me. Since I'm not a man of God, I'm not as adept at turning the other cheek as you are. Good day to you, Miss Catherine."

"Good day, Professor Foley." She bobbed a curtsy.

Grasping his cane, he went down the steps and headed up the street to round the corner in the direction of the university.

Ignoring the rabble, Jack descended the steps, his grip on Cathy's arm tightening as he headed them toward the manse next door. Head held high, his daughter marched by his side. He marveled at this child with whom he'd been blessed. Not only was she beautiful, she also had courage and dignity.

Another object hurtled through the air. With a cry, his daughter slumped against him. He caught her in his arms before she could fall to the ground. A fist-sized rock quivered on the road beside them.

****

"Will she recover?" Reverend Jack Wallace stood at the end of his daughter's bed and waited for the doctor's verdict.

"I won't make rash promises, John." The gray-haired physician heaved a sigh as he stood from where he'd been sitting on the edge of the unconscious girl's bed. A thick bandage had been wound about her head. "She's taken a serious blow to the temple. The next few hours will tell."

"This is my fault." Jack threw back his head and closed his eyes. "I shouldn't have allowed her to go to church this morning. I knew some members of my congregation were at odds with what they discovered I'd been doing. The sins of the fathers…"

"Some have gone so far as to brand you a heretic." Doctor Blake picked up his bag and headed for the door.

"And you, Nelson? What is your opinion?" Jack opened his eyes to face the man squarely.

"John, you've been treading on dangerous ground. Perhaps if you'd managed to keep it quiet, if your congregation hadn't found out…"

"Nelson, I'm asking for your personal opinion."

"Very well." The doctor heaved a sigh. "I think you should be free to do as you please, but knowing this community as well as I do, I realize your actions have rendered it impossible for you to redeem yourself among its people. If I were you, I'd leave…go somewhere rogues such as yourself are tolerated, quite possibly even accepted. I'll be back tomorrow to check on Miss Cathy. Good day to you, Reverend Wallace."

He picked up his black bag and left the room.

Chapter Two

Lottie opened her eyes and blinked in the shaft of sunlight.

Where am I? How did I get here?

Slowly becoming aware of her surroundings, she realized she was in a wide, luxurious bed, its sheets and pillows soft and clean. As her scope of comprehension widened, she became aware that she was in a large chamber, high-ceilinged, with fine furnishings and two tall, elegantly curtained windows letting in a gush of sunlight. A young woman in the garb of a housemaid was briskly folding fresh linen at the far side of the room.

"Good morning." Lottie struggled to speak, but the words came out as a harsh croak.

"You're awake." The maid hastened to her bedside, a smile lighting up her plump, pretty face. "His lordship will be that pleased."

"His lordship?" Again that strange-sounding voice she realized had to be her own.

"Sir Jeffrey, him what brought you here. I must fetch him. He left strict orders that I was to tell him the minute you came back to us."

She hustled out of the room before Lottie could question her further.

The servant had said, "Sir Jeffrey." She struggled at the fog in her mind. The coach. Strong arms lifting her. Being wrapped in the warmth of soft wool.

And then nothing. For a long time, nothing. How long had she been unaware…?

"So you're back with us." A man's voice, bright with enthusiasm, made her flinch. Gingerly turning her head toward the sound, she saw a tall male figure entering the room and advancing toward the bed. "Excellent, excellent."

Perfectly groomed and dressed in the height of fashion, he had a handsome face, broad shoulders, and a self-assured attitude. *An aristocrat.*

"Dr. Coat has visited and declared that all you need is rest and care. I can assure you of both. Now what may I do for you this fine morning? What do you require?"

"Your name." She forced the request over bone-dry lips and mouth.

"Of course. Where are my manners? Jeffrey Tinsdale, your servant, ma'am." He bowed. "And yours?"

She hesitated. Her thoughts were clearing, remembrance and fear returning.

"Charlotte…Charlotte Dally."

"I'm delighted to make your acquaintance, Miss Dally. It is miss?" He raised an eyebrow.

"Yes."

"And so, Miss Dally, is there someone I should notify on your behalf? Someone who will be relieved to know you're alive and recovering?"

"No." The word came out more sharply than she intended as memory after memory tumbled back into her mind. Then, more softly, "No one."

"Very well then." His expression held only a slight

hesitation before he continued. "You will remain with us. Lilly will to see to your needs. She's an excellent lady's maid. She tended to my…wife."

"Tended?"

"My wife died a year ago." He turned and went to stare out the window. "She was run down by a carriage…much as I suspect you were."

"I'm sorry."

So he thinks I've been run down by a carriage. I won't have to explain further.

"Thank you." He swung back to face her, a weak smile on his lips, his eyes too bright. "Now"—he revived his former cheerful outlook—"I must be off. Good day to you, Miss Charlotte Dally."

After he'd gone, Lottie looked across the room toward the long windows and saw her satin gown hanging over the back of a chair. It was torn and stained, barely recognizable as the elegant garment it had once been.

"I'm afraid your lovely dress is ruined, miss." The maid, catching her gaze, paused in her work. "I thought to try to clean and repair it, but on close examination, I realized it was hopeless."

"Yes…yes, I can see that it is quite beyond fixing." As she stared at it, all the horrors of the previous night filtered back to her…the fire, her tenants' screams, hands grabbing her, fists and boots pummeling her until she lost consciousness, coming back to life lying in the street in excruciating pain.

And then the man, this Sir Jeffrey Tinsdale, finding her and taking her into his carriage. Once again, she'd lapsed into nothingness until this morning.

But why had she slept so long? Who had undressed

her, put her into a fine linen night shift, ensconced her in this luxurious bed?

As if guessing her questions, the maid came close to the bed and smiled down at her.

"You've nothing to fear from anyone in this house," she soothed. "Sir Jeffrey ordered the doctor fetched at once as he carried you inside. When Doctor Coat arrived and saw your condition, he immediately gave you a hearty dose of something called laudanum. It allowed me to remove your clothing and wash your wounds without causing you more discomfort. It worked its magic, because you stayed asleep until just now." Her eyes suddenly filled with tears. "Whoever did this to you, miss, should be drawn and quartered, and no mistake. Imagine a carriage driver running you down and then leaving you to suffer in the cold and wet."

Touched by the young woman's concern, Lottie reached out a bruised, scraped hand. After a slight hesitation, Lilly took it in hers. They smiled at each other.

"Now, miss, I must get on with the day." Lilly drew herself up and once again became the efficient servant. "I'll be fetching your breakfast. Dr. Coat said we must get your strength back."

She swung away and left the room. Lottie was left with an overwhelming sense of how fortunate she'd been.

****

Later, after Lilly had fetched her a light breakfast as ordered by the doctor, Lottie, supported by pillows, put her teacup back in its saucer on the tray before her and decided it was time to learn more about her rescuer.

"Lilly," she addressed the young woman working about the room. "Have you been with your master—Sir Jeffrey—long?" Her voice still sounded gravelly, but the tea and food had given her sufficient strength to talk, and she wanted to know more of the circumstances in which she found herself.

"Since his marriage five years ago." Lilly turned and smiled at Lottie. "I came here as lady's maid to his wife, Lady Alise." At the mention of her former mistress, the young woman's eyes watered a little.

"They were a happy couple?" Lottie caught herself asking. Longing for more knowledge of the man who'd taken her in made her curious.

"Oh, my, yes, miss." Lilly came to the bed, a smile making rainbows of her unshed tears. "They loved each other so very much. When she was killed, I feared for a while he'd choose to follow her to the grave." She turned away, swiping a hand over her eyes. "Now I must be off. The nightshift you're wearing is one that belonged to Lady Alise. Sir Jeffrey has given me the task of finding clothing for you from her wardrobe." She picked up the tattered dress from the chair. "I'll just be disposing of this."

"Yes, dispose of it…please." Lottie suppressed a shudder. She wanted it gone, along with the terrible memories it held.

"Is there some house I should visit to pick up your personal things?" Lilly paused at the door. Her eyes asked a question that went much deeper.

"No…no house." She avoided the maid's eyes. She couldn't blame the young woman for seeking to know more about this mysterious woman whom her master had brought in out of the night.

"Very well, miss. I'll just see to finding more clothing for you." She turned and left the room.

Alone, Lottie took the time to reflect. Douglas would have helped her, but in fear of losing his life, he'd fled to British North America, to a place called Riverhaven. Other than the tall, handsome young outlaw, she realized she knew of no one who would be willing to assist her, and he was too far away to come to her aid.

She'd have to rely on the kindness of Sir Jeffrey Tinsdale…at least temporarily.

Chapter Three

Reverend Jack Wallace sat in the chair beside his daughter's bed and bowed his head in prayer. He'd tried not to ask the Lord for too many favors over his lifetime, but now he couldn't refrain.

An image of her trying to protect a donkey a farmer had been abusing in the town street flashed into his mind. She'd rushed at the man, seizing his arm before he could again bring down the whip on the little animal's bleeding flanks.

Much as it went against his abhorrence of cruelty to animals, he'd had to intervene. The law of the land declared the donkey was the man's property to do with as he pleased. Jack couldn't allow his daughter to be arrested for her protest.

"That's right, *Reverend*," the farmer had yelled after Jack as he drew his protesting child away. "Take you and your ungodly ways off! We don't need such as you in our town!"

Jack shook his head. Bad enough that most of the community had declared him to be a heretic and a sinner, but to lump Cathy into the mix scoured him to the core.

"There's a letter come for you." Breaking into his thoughts, his housekeeper, Hannah Keen, waddled into the room and thrust the sealed paper at him. He noted she no longer referred to him as "Reverend" or even

"Mr. Wallace." He strongly suspected she was the person who had uncovered his activities at the university and not hesitated to make it general knowledge.

Quite possibly his lack of romantic interest in her twenty-eight-year-old daughter had contributed to her change in attitude toward him. Where once she'd been obliging almost to the point of simpering, after he'd as gently as possibly rebuked Maud Keen's advances, his housekeeper had become sly and underhanded.

He suspected she remained in his employ on the hope of gathering demeaning information. He longed to dismiss her, but he didn't know where he could find a replacement at the wages he was able to pay. Furthermore, Cathy needed a woman in her life.

"Thank you, Mrs. Keen." He accepted the communication. He made no move to open it while the rotund woman stood, hands clasped over her protruding stomach, watching. Its seal told him its source, and he had no desire for the woman to learn of its contents. "Miss Cathy needs fresh bedding. Will you see to it?"

With a grunt, she turned and left the room. He drew a deep breath. Though it went against everything he taught and believed, he admitted he was still struggling to forgive the woman for what he believed she'd done, how she'd destroyed his life, but most of all what her vicious tongue had done to Cathy. Cathy who innocently admired her father, Cathy who believed in him with all her heart and soul.

No point in putting it off. He broke the official seal, drew a deep breath, and began to read.

So. That is how it's to be.

A sardonic gesture curled a corner of his mouth.

"Papa?"

His daughter's voice jerked him out of his thoughts. He vaulted forward to kneel by her bed. Relief flooding through his soul, he looked into her blue eyes for the first time since she'd been struck by the rock an hour earlier.

"Cathy." He caught her hand in his and stared at her for a moment before bowing his head. "Thank you, God, most humbly, thank you."

"What happened, Papa?" Her words were weak, barely above a whisper, but she was speaking, and for that he was more deeply grateful than he could describe.

"An accident, my love. Dr. Coat says you'll be right as rain in no time. Now you have to rest. And take nourishment." He kissed her cheek and stood. "I'll have Mrs. Keen bring you some broth."

"Papa, what is that paper in your hand?" She gestured weakly.

"Nothing…nothing that should concern you at the moment. We'll discuss it later." He turned and left the room. He'd wait until she was stronger to share the document's contents with her. Right now, she needed something good. He knew just what that would be.

****

"Come." He smiled at Cathy, where she sat before the fire in the small room they called a parlor, and held out his hand. "I have a surprise for you."

"What is it?" She got to her feet, and he strode to assist her.

"Papa, please," she protested, "it's been three days since the accident. I'm quite recovered. The doctor has said as much."

"Very well." He led the way to the front door, then held it open for her to precede him outside.

Tied to a spreading maple in the manse's front yard was a small donkey.

"Oh, Papa!" she breathed. "What...?"

"She's yours. That is, if you want her. Apparently, she's too small to do the work Farmer Jones needs done."

She rushed down the steps to throw her arms about the little animal's neck.

"Thank you, thank you, Papa!" When she finally released the donkey, she looked up at her father on the steps, her eyes glowing. "I shall call her Grace because she was saved by grace and you." She returned her attention to the animal. "No one will ever, ever whip you again, Grace."

"I think that's a fine name." He advanced to the pair. "I'll put her in the stable with Glory. Our mare will be glad to have company. And you, young lady..." He untied the animal and turned toward the barn. "Get back inside, out of the cold. It may be spring, but in this country, that northeast wind makes it still feel like winter."

"Yes, Papa." She started to obey, then swung back to embrace her father. "You're the best father ever."

Jack Wallace swallowed hard as he watched her go back up the manse steps and wave, a smile brightening her face like a ray of sunshine before she vanished inside.

"And you're the best daughter," he breathed as he led the donkey to the barn.

****

"Papa, how?" Cathy asked the question when he

returned to the manse to find her once more sitting before the fire in the parlor.

"How? What are you talking about, child?" He deliberately used the term to tease her. At sixteen, she no longer considered herself a child. And perhaps rightly so. He'd officiated at services where the bride was no older.

"How did you manage to get Grace? I know Farmer Jones wouldn't give her to you, the old curmudgeon." She stood and went to him.

"Cathy Wallace, that's most unchristian of you. Liam Jones is a hardworking…"

"You went back to blacksmithing, didn't you?" Grasping his right hand, she looked down at it, then up at her father. Her eyes widened with accusation. "Papa, you're an educated man, you shouldn't…"

"You know I was apprenticed to a blacksmith as a boy. A little manual labor never hurt anyone. Furthermore, it was only for a day. Farmer Jones didn't want much for the donkey. He called her useless, a waste of hay. Seeing that little creature freed from abuse was well worth a few hours at the forge. Now…" He kissed the top of her head. "I have a homily to write, even if my congregation might only be you and Theodore."

Chapter Four

"Ah, Lilly told me you were up and about." Sir Jeffrey strode across her bedchamber to stand before her as she sat in a chair in front of the fire blazing on the hearth. "Wonderful, wonderful. I take it you're feeling much better?"

She smiled up at him. "Much."

It had been two days since her arrival in his home, and she believed she was well on the road to recovery. A visit from Dr. Coat that morning had confirmed her return to health. He'd allowed Lilly to help her out of bed and into a chair. That evening, wrapped in a warm cashmere dressing gown covering a silk night shift, a cup of tea steaming in her hands, Lottie felt ensconced in luxury.

"Excellent." He indicated the chair opposite hers. "May I?"

"Of course."

"I haven't visited you since your first day here," he explained, settling himself comfortably. "I wanted to give you time to recuperate. I have, however, kept close tabs on your recovery through Lilly. I trust her services, and indeed, everything has been to your satisfaction?"

"I could not have asked to be treated better." She paused before continuing. "Sir Jeffrey, I fear I've been negligent in properly thanking you for rescuing me. Saving me probably cost you an evening's entertainment with friends."

"Hardly." He smiled ruefully. "I was on my way home from an unpleasant dinner with a group of army officers and government officials. I've been sent up here to Scotland to inspect their activities and report back to the prime minister. I fear my views on British treatment of the Highlanders is at variance with those of the gentlemen with whom I shared the evening." He continued with a sigh. "After the meal, as whisky circulated more and more freely, I fast became the object of verbal attacks."

"How unfortunate…but it is heartening to hear of an English official who has the welfare of Highlanders in mind," she remarked, her respect for the man escalating.

"I only wish I could do more for those poor souls who are being driven from their homes to make way for sheep." His words took on a sadly wistful tone. "I visited a few of their humble dwellings…black houses, they're called…three rooms only, with their livestock actually occupying the first, and the other two used for all other family needs. I met one woman in a small village with four small children clinging to her skirts. Her husband had not returned from tending their sheep…she suspected he'd been killed…and her home had been burned. With nowhere to go, all five were on the verge of starvation."

"How awful!"

"I managed to get her a small hut on the bank of a stream not far from the village and provide a store of food, but how she'll manage a winter…" His voice trailed off, and he looked down at his hands.

"You did what you could." Her words were soft,

warm with feelings for a man she recognized as a truly good individual.

"But it's not enough." He looked up at her, his eyes bright with a mission. "When I get back to England, I intend to petition the Prime Minister—the King, if needs be—to stop this persecution of these innocent people. They no more represent the threat of an uprising than the animals they tend."

"Nevertheless, on behalf of my country's people, I thank you for your efforts…past, present, and in the future. Sir Jeffrey…" She hesitated. "You've not asked any questions about me…who I actually am, why I have no one you should notify."

"Troubling you with such matters at this time wouldn't speed your recovery." He stood. "Perhaps you will tell me some day, perhaps not. I will leave that up to your discretion." He stood and left the room.

A truly amazing man. Lottie sipped her tea, knowing how fortunate she'd been to be in his care.

****

This was to prove the first of regular evening visits to Lottie's room. When he did not have official duties, he joined her before the fire and, as her health improved, shared brandy with her.

Lottie enjoyed chatting with him. They talked of everything from politics to the weather, from his avid interest in fine horses to the latest trends in fashion, some of which both found amusing. Through it all, Sir Jeffrey had proven himself a gentleman to the core.

****

"I've had news from England." Frowning, he looked down at his hands where he'd clasped them in his lap as he sat with her before the fire in her room. It was a fortnight after she'd come to live in his house. "I'm being recalled." He glanced up at her. "Do you think you will be up to travelling in a few days?"

"Sir Jeffrey, you've been most kind." Now that she was feeling better, she realized the inappropriateness of their continuing a relationship, of her remaining in his home. "There's no need for you to continue to care for me."

"Perhaps no need as you see it, but from my point of view there is." He paused. "Miss Dally…Charlotte… you've provided excellent company for me. I've been a lonely man since my wife's death. I'd be deeply indebted to you for continuing to be my companion… my platonic companion."

The intense sincerity in his eyes caught at her heart. Here was a good man, a decent man, a man who'd saved her life, asking her to be his friend. How could she refuse?

A second thought, purely selfish, invaded her mind. Going to England would take her out of the reaches of *them*.

"Very well, Sir Jeffrey. I will accompany you to England…on one condition."

"Name it."

"That you will never question me about my past nor try to delve into it." She met his eyes squarely, her heartbeat quickening.

He hesitated, a slight frown crinkling his forehead.

She rushed ahead. "Of course, if such is too much a demand, I shall leave before you start your journey south."

"No, no." He was instantly adamant. "Certainly not. Your past shall be truly in the past. Oh, and I also have a condition." He was smiling at her, the kindly, wonderful smile she'd come to know and enjoy.

"Which is?"

"That you cease to call me Sir Jeffrey. Make it Jeffrey only, please."

"Very well." She smiled back. "Jeffrey…and Charlotte it shall be."

"Thank you." He stood. "Now I must begin to make arrangements for our departure. Lilly, of course, will accompany us as chaperone and to see to your needs."

Chapter Five

Lottie stared about the vast, handsome foyer of the house. If the grounds and outside of the manor had impressed her, its interior did so doubly. Sir Jeffrey Tinsdale had to be a very wealthy man.

"Chambers, we'll have tea in the morning room," he instructed the formal-looking butler who'd greeted them at the door.

"Of course, sir." He took Sir Jeffrey's hat and gloves, bowed, and hastened off.

"Come along." Her host, at her elbow, urged her to a doorway at the left. "You must rest while Lilly makes your bedchamber comfortable. Lilly...?" He turned to the young woman who'd followed them carrying a small valise. "Miss Charlotte will be using the blue room. You know what must be done."

"Yes, sir." She bobbed a curtsy and headed up the wide, curving staircase before them.

"Jeffrey, I'm really quite all right," Lottie protested as he guided her into a beautifully decorated room with wide windows letting in a gush of sunlight. A fire crackled on the hearth. "I assure you I'm not in need of rest...or nourishment."

"Perhaps you're not, but I most certainly am." He handed her into a chair in front of the fire before sitting down opposite her. "Once we're sufficiently refreshed, I have something I wish to show you...to introduce you

22

to."

When they'd finished eating, he stood and held down a hand to her. "Have you the strength to accompany me to the stables?"

"Yes, of course." Puzzled by his choice of walks, she got to her feet, adjusted her hat, and took the arm he offered to her.

Once inside the well-kept stables, with stable boys bowing before him, Sir Jeffrey led her to a box stall near its center. A tall, muscular man inside was busily brushing one of the most beautiful horses Lottie had ever seen. Its coat was golden, its flowing mane and tail snow white as were its hooves and facial blaze.

"Biggs, this is Miss Charlotte Dally," Jeffrey introduced her. "Charlotte, this is my head groom, Harvey Biggs."

"Your servant, miss." The big man touched his forelock.

"I'm hoping she and Beauty will become friends," Sir Jeffrey continued. "Please bring Beauty out into the walkway, that they might better become acquainted."

The man obeyed. The mare was indeed aptly named. Carefully Lottie reached out a gloved hand to touch the golden neck. The animal turned her head and blew softly.

"She likes you, miss." Biggs nodded approval. "Come to her head. Never fear. She's gentle as a kitten."

She followed the groom's instruction. The mare nuzzled against Lottie.

"Very good." Sir Jeffrey was smiling at them.

"She's right partial to ladies, miss." Biggs continued to hold the rope attached to the mare's halter.

"And right lonely since…" He stopped speaking and lowered his head.

"Yes, she has been." Sir Jeffrey spoke softly, then raised his tone as he smiled at Lottie. "But that is in the past. Miss Charlotte, will you befriend this creature?"

"Of course." Involved in enjoying the mare's attention, she responded quickly, but then continued more slowly, "However, that might not be fair to her. I don't know how long I shall be here."

"Not something with which to concern ourselves at the moment." Jeffrey dismissed her comment with a bright remark. "Do you ride?"

"Yes."

"Would you like to do so again? I assure you Beauty is as kindly and gentle a mount as you'll find anywhere in England."

"I'd love to." She turned to him with a delighted smile.

"Would you be wanting me to help the lady?" Biggs looked over at his master. "I…"

"No, thank you, Biggs. I'll be accompanying Miss Dally. Please make arrangements to have the mare and my horse saddled and ready each morning at nine o'clock."

"Aye, sir." A sudden hint of a Highland accent flashed into the groom's speech and with it a spurt of remembrance of another Highlander into her mind…one who had been her friend and guardian all those months ago. Where was he now? Was he alive or dead? Would she ever know?

Chapter Six

Reverend Jack Wallace walked into the stable behind the manse where his daughter stood involved in brushing the donkey's rough coat. He could put it off no longer. He had to tell her the truth.

"She's looking lovely, isn't she, Papa?" Cathy turned to her father, a bright smile lighting up her pretty face.

"Indeed, she is." He went to place a hand on the little animal's flank where a whip wound was healing due to the young woman's care. "Cathy, I must talk to you."

"Of course." She paused in her grooming and looked at him. "Papa, what is it?" Her smile faded. "What has happened? You're not ill, are you?" Distress flooded over her countenance.

"No, definitely not." He caught her hand holding the brush in his and took it from her. Her mother's catastrophic illness still flooded to the front of her mind, he knew, whenever he had so much as a cold. He led her to a bench against the wall. "Sit, please."

He hated the way her eyes had widened, her face blanched. Best get to it right away.

"I've been given a new pastoral charge. We'll have to move."

"Oh." The relief in her voice astonished him. "Is that all?"

"It's some distance from here...near the New Brunswick coast, in the community of Riverhaven. I understand it's only a village, with lumbermills and shipbuilding...no schools or libraries such as you've enjoyed here in Fredericton. In fact, the manse is on farm land which the former pastor cultivated to supplement his income..."

"How wonderful!" She burst into his description. "A farm! A place no doubt with a fenced pasture where Grace and Glory can run free! I can have chickens, and maybe a goat..."

"Cathy, I'm not sure you fully understand." He hated to quell her enthusiasm. "From what I gather, this Riverhaven is a rough place full of lumbermen and laborers and, I've been given to understand, more than a few not entirely law-abiding citizens..."

"Who need a minister such as yourself. Papa, is that all you had to tell me? I thought your news was going to be dire. I shall be glad to move to this Riverhaven."

Her tone lost some of its glow as she came to the end of her speech.

"Cathy, what is it? Don't tell me you won't miss your friends."

"No, I shan't." She stood and returned to brushing Grace, her shoulders set in a defiantly rigid stance. "They're nothing to me...not any longer."

"Oh." He drew a deep breath.

She didn't have to explain. He'd noticed how the other girls of the community, girls Cathy had considered friends, had begun to distance themselves from her. And he knew why. Parents didn't want their daughters associating with the child of a man they'd branded an atheist, a heretic, and a sinner.

"Well, then, we'll be on our way by week's end." He slapped his hands on his thighs and stood. "That is, if you can be ready by then," he finished with less enthusiasm.

"I can be ready by morning, if needs be." She gave the donkey a few more brush strokes before turning to her father, concern knitting a frown between her eyebrows. "But do you think Glory will be able to transport our belongings all the way to Riverhaven? She's getting old, Papa, and…"

"She'll manage." He went into the stall to pat the elderly mare's graying coat. "Remember, we haven't all that much to move. The furnishings in the manse belong to the church. All we'll be taking are our personal items. And my books. There's no immediate rush. We'll let Glory choose our pace."

"Yes, of course." His daughter brightened. "And when we get to our new home, Glory will have an actual pasture to enjoy. I'll go inside and start packing at once."

Chapter Seven

Lottie sat at the foot of the long dining table and looked up its length at Sir Jeffrey in the master's seat. When she'd assured him she was feeling much better, he'd invited her to join him for dinner downstairs. Lilly had been quick to respond with a beautiful gown of blue silk and the offer to dress her hair.

"You're making the master happy as I've not seen him since Lady Alise's death," she'd said as she arranged Lottie's curls. "And that makes me happy."

But not everyone in the household felt as her lady's maid did. Chambers, the butler, appeared struggling to be polite, and Mrs. Willowby, the housekeeper, treated her with ill-disguised disdain. Even Roger, the footman serving at the table, regarded her at times with a sly grin. No one in the household aside from Lilly accepted her willingly into the company of their master.

"Perhaps my joining you for dinner isn't wise," Lottie remarked when Sir Jeffrey joined her in the drawing room after their third dinner together. "I don't think your servants regard it as appropriate."

"Nonsense." He seated himself across from her before the fire. "You have the manners and deportment of a lady." He paused before continuing, "At any rate, it's not their place to decide what is proper. This is my house."

"But Jeffrey, I don't want to cause trouble between

28

you and your staff. Having Lilly bring meals to my room…"

"No." The word came out sharply, and he was quick to modify his tone. "No. I am master here, and I want you to dine with me." He paused before continuing, his tone solicitous. "That is, unless it makes you uncomfortable. Then, of course…"

"If you enjoy my presence, then I shall continue to dine with you." She smiled over at him. "You've been so kind. If there's anything within my power to repay you, then I shall."

"Excellent." He reached for his glass and took a sip. "It's settled. Now to other matters. Tomorrow I must go to London. If there's anything you desire, please inform Lilly. She's a fine young woman, and I can tell already she's devoted to you."

****

The next morning Lottie, clad in a simple muslin dress, managed to slip out of the house and make her way to the stable.

The stable lads greeted her with a respectful touching of caps and forelocks, but she caught a few sly smiles among them.

They think I'm their master's mistress.

Realizing there was nothing she could do about it, she passed them by with smiling dignity as she made her way to the palomino mare's stall. She was reaching through the bars to rub the animal's nose when Harvey Biggs' voice made her turn.

"She's a fine lady," he said nodding toward the mare. "One of the best I've ever had under my care."

"She's beautiful and apparently possessed of a kindly spirit," Lottie responded, smiling at the head groom.

"Aye, but she's been missing Lady Alise," he replied, his tone reflecting respect for the woman. "They were quite a pair, I can tell you. Here…" He opened the stall door and stepped inside. "Let me bring her."

Shortly he had the animal in the crossties in the walkway. Lottie moved to her head and caressed the soft nose.

"You are a lovely creature." She spoke softly. "I hope you and I will be friends."

In response, Beauty rubbed against her and wheezed a soft sigh.

"Aye, there." The groom stood back, a broad smile coming to his face. "Just what the lass needed. Another lass to share her time."

****

"Are you quite sure this is what your master wishes me to wear?" Lottie stared at the luxurious green velvet riding habit Lilly held before her.

"Quite sure, miss." She swung the garment about, her expression softening. "Lady Alise looked so beautiful in it. I'm sure you will as well. It will please Sir Jeffrey to see you wearing it." She hesitated before continuing cautiously, "You don't look unlike her."

"Very well." Lottie could not deny the man who'd saved her life anything within her power that he desired, but the maid's words troubled her. Was he perhaps seeing her as a substitute for his deceased wife?

When she'd finished dressing, she paused to survey herself in the cheval mirror near a window. She looked well, she thought, adjusting the perky little green hat perched on her curls. But her feet…she looked down at them encased in satin slippers.

"Here." Lilly stood beside her holding out a pair of gleaming black riding boots. "Try them, miss. I'm suspecting they might just fit."

Lottie seated herself in a chair and allowed the maid to pull them on. They fitted perfectly. Standing, Lottie looked down at them, the uneasy feeling that she was moving into another woman's life increasing at a troubling rate.

Soon she was advancing down the wide staircase. Garbed in riding clothing, Sir Jeffrey waited for her at its foot. His eyes widened as he saw her.

"You look lovely, my dear, absolutely lovely." He took her arm as she reached the bottom. His smile left no doubt as to his delight. "You will appear ready to have your portrait taken once you're mounted on Beauty."

"Oh, my, such a lovely compliment." Reflexively, she cast him one of the intimate sideways smiles that were second nature to her.

"Nothing more than the truth." Wetting his lips, he cleared his throat. "Come along now." He urged her toward the door. "Biggs has our horses waiting."

Damn! I've made him uneasy. Get a grip, Lottie Danvers.

****

Over the following days, he welcomed her each morning for their ride. She enjoyed the outings and, once he was convinced of her return to health, he allowed her to accompany him on his round of estate inspections.

"You're amazing, Miss Charlotte," he exclaimed as they halted near a stream one bright spring morning to

31

allow their mounts to drink. His countenance was alive with pleasure. "It appears you were born to ride."

The soft inquiry at the end of his words caught at her. He'd been amazingly silent in asking her about her past. Now this gentle remark made her realize he was becoming curious. How could she blame him?

She gave a noncommittal response. "I've had some experience." Beauty lifted her head from the water just then, and Lottie said, "Now we'd best be getting back. Did you not tell me you had a meeting with your steward this morning?"

"Forgive me." He was immediately contrite. "I've promised not to pry. Yes, we should be getting back." He turned his mount about. "Are you up to a canter?"

Chapter Eight

Two mornings later, when Lottie came down dressed for riding, she didn't find Sir Jeffrey waiting for her in his usual place near the front entrance.

"Chambers, where is Sir Jeffrey?" she asked as the butler appeared from the rear of the manor.

"He's been delayed, miss. He's asked that you join him in his office." He held out a hand to indicate the way.

At the door of the room to which Chambers led her, she paused. Seated behind an impressive oak desk, Jeffrey was involved in a conversation with Adams, his steward, who stood bent over him. Open before them was a strongbox.

"I'll be keeping some funds here in a top drawer, Adams," he said indicating the right-hand side of his desk. "Biggs will be needing funds to pay for harness he's ordered, and I don't want to have to bother opening the safe. I also have a few other paltry expenses that need seeing to shortly. You can put the rest away."

He took a handful of bank notes as well as a quantity of gold coins from the container and placed them into the drawer.

"Very good." The steward picked up the strongbox and crossed the room to place it inside an open safe.

"Ah, Charlotte." Having finished his business, Sir

Jeffrey looked up and smiled. "Excuse me for keeping you waiting."

He stood and crossed the room to take her arm. As they headed out of the manor, Lottie thought how very trusting was the man accompanying her, to leave a considerable amount of money in a desk drawer.

Or perhaps, she thought on reflection, he had an entirely devoted and trustworthy staff.

****

"It's right pretty, isn't it, mistress?" Her eyes bright with admiration, Lilly held up the gown. "You'll be the envy of all the ladies at the ball."

"I don't understand." Lottie stared at the elegant creation.

"His lordship had it made up for the fancy dress ball next week. You're to go as some queen from foreign parts."

"But how did he know my measurements? Surely a seamstress with the skill to make such a garment would not dare to attempt it without exact specifications."

"Surely, miss, you must realize you're the exact same size as Lady Alise." Lilly looked at her, surprised. "You've been wearing her clothes, even her boots and shoes, and they fit like they were made for you. Madame Gabrielle simply made this gown to the specifications she had for her ladyship."

"What do you think?" Sir Jeffrey strode into the room, smiling. "You shall be the envy of all at the event. I only hope I will prove a fitting courier."

"Jeffrey, I cannot possibly accompany you. It's not appropriate..." Memories flooded back.

"Charlotte, please." He came to take her hands. "You'd be doing me a great honor."

Looking up into his imploring, kindly expression, Lottie drew a deep breath. She owed this man her life.

"Very well, Jeffrey."

"Wonderful. Lilly, see that Miss Charlotte's hair is dressed appropriately. It will be an outstanding evening."

His pleasure beaming, he hesitated, paused a moment, then bent forward to bestow a quick kiss on her cheek before striding out of the room.

Her hand flew to the place where his lips had touched her skin. Looking at the luxurious gown, she wondered if its purchase had been one of the so-called paltry expenses that had induced Jeffrey to keep money in his desk drawer.

****

"I'm so happy to be out of Scotland." The sound of the woman's voice sent a shocking chill racing over Lottie with its familiarity.

She'd been enjoying a quiet moment of refreshment near opened French doors when she overheard two women begin a conversation beyond a large potted plant to her left.

"My dear, I don't know how you stood all those months in that dreadful backwater. I realize Edinburgh has a sizeable English population, but still…"

"Yes, but not anyone of note. My husband found ways to amuse himself for a time, but I put an end to those pleasures the moment I learned he'd begun dragging our son along on his debauched adventures."

Nauseous, her head beginning to spin with a horrible sense of unreality, Lottie put out a hand to steady herself against a pillar. Memories of that horrible night in the gutter in the rain, of that same voice…

"Well, enough about that ungodly place," the woman's companion murmured. "Who is the creature Lord Tinsdale is escorting? Did you notice the tantalizing way she moves, the manner in which, even behind a mask, she manages to cast him provocative looks? Jeffrey may try to pass her off as a visiting cousin, but that's obviously a lie."

"Jeffrey has been on his own much too long," the horribly recognizable voice drawled. "It's high time Janet got herself back from cavorting about Italy. If she wants to secure him and his wealth, she'd best make a serious move…and soon."

In a haze of terror, Lottie stumbled out through the opened French doors into the night and fell back to lean against the cold stones of the manor wall. Panic seized her. She had to get away before the midnight unmasking.

"Charlotte, my dear, I've been searching for you." His voice made her flinch. Jeffrey was beside her, holding out a glass of champagne. "My God, what is it? You look positively ill."

She grasped the drink from his hand, quaffed it down, and handed the empty glass back to him.

"Jeffrey, we must go," she whispered hoarsely. "Immediately."

"Of course, if you wish." Concern resonated through his words. In the moonlight she saw his brow furrowing. "You, there!" He hailed a servant passing inside the open doorway. "Order Sir Jeffrey Tinsdale's carriage at once."

The man bowed his acquiescence and hurried off.

"Come." He took her arm and moved to draw her back inside the ballroom. "I'll find you a place to rest…"

"Jeffrey, no!" She planted her feet. Realizing her refusal must seem suspiciously dramatic, she forced a faint smile. "The night air is refreshing. Can we not walk around the house to the carriage?"

"Certainly." He sounded puzzled but didn't argue. His hand beneath her elbow, he led her along the walk to the front of the manor. Once there, he found a bench for her while they awaited the carriage.

As an involuntary shiver shook her, he pulled off his coat. Placing it gently about her, he called to a footman standing nearby. "Miss Charlotte Dally's wrap. Fetch it, and be quick about it."

Jeffrey's tone had snapped from compassionate to authoritative. The man dashed off.

"I'm sorry, my dear." In the light of the torches blazing nearby, he frowned down at her. "It was thoughtless of me to bring you here. You're still not strong."

"There is no need to apologize." Lottie found her equilibrium returning now she was out of range of that woman. "Perhaps I've imbibed too much champagne."

"Yes, perhaps." She caught the skepticism in his voice. After all, he'd just seen her quaff an entire glass of wine without so much as an eye blink, sneeze, or cough.

She closed her eyes and tried to fathom what she had to do.

As the carriage arrived and Sir Jeffrey solicitously helped her inside, she came to a decision…a decision that hurt her to the core.

Chapter Eight

"Charlotte, what are you doing?" Sir Jeffrey entered her room the following morning to discover her in a flurry of packing. Lilly, looking hurt and confused, assisted her.

"Jeffrey, I can't stay here any longer." Lottie continued to fold clothing into a small trunk. Beside it, a valise lay open, toilet articles visible inside. "I'll send payment for what I'm taking as soon as I'm settled and have found gainful employment."

"Charlotte, this makes no sense." He moved to stand close to her, to block her path from the armoire to the trunk. "Have I done something to offend you?"

"No, Jeffrey, certainly not."

"You may go, Lilly." Sir Jeffrey, becoming aware of the maid's interest, dismissed the servant in a tone sharper than Lottie had ever heard him use.

Lilly, after a quick glance at Lottie, bobbed a curtsy and scuttled out of the room.

"Charlotte, you must tell me. What is the reason for this sudden desire to leave? If I've offended you in any way, I do most humbly beg your pardon."

"Of course you haven't. Jeffrey, you've been nothing but kind to me."

"Then, why?" His expression of hurt confusion cut her to the bone.

"Jeffrey, the last thing I want to do is hurt you. It's

for that very reason I must leave."

"I'm still confused…"

"Last night, at the ball, I overheard two ladies gossiping." She eased past him to lay a gown on the bed. "They spoke of your attachment to a lady named Janet. They wondered what she will think when she arrives home from Italy next month and discovers this so-called cousin sharing your hearth and home."

"Pointless tittle-tattle! Definitely no reason for all of this!" He swung his arm to indicate the packing.

"Then you deny a relationship with Janet…that she's not, in fact, your fiancée?"

"Yes…no…that is, there is no formal commitment between us. Our names have been linked through wishful thinking on the part of her mother. The Wyse family fortunes have become strained. I believe Lady Millicent sees a marriage between her daughter and me as a solution. I assure you, I have no intention of being seduced into a family of fortune hunters. Charlotte…" He caught her by the shoulders. "A bit of gossip is not sufficient reason…"

"Jeffrey, I must." A bitter ache in her soul, she put a hand gently on his jaw.

Looking deep into her eyes, he hesitated a moment before releasing her and dropping on one knee before her. He clutched her hands in his.

"Marry me, Charlotte." He looked up at her, the blatant sincerity in his eyes tearing at her heart. "You'll want for nothing it's in my power to provide. I promise to protect you with every ounce of my strength…"

"Jeffrey, please!" She drew him to his feet. "You mustn't offer marriage. You don't know me. You don't know my past."

"I know I've never been happier than when I'm with you." He sucked in a deep breath. "I know I love you with all my heart."

"No, no, no!" Fighting tears, she swung away, turning her back to him.

"Charlotte!" She felt his hands once again on her shoulders, kind, gentle hands, the same hands that had rescued her from the gutter that awful March evening. "Charlotte, at least think about what you're planning to do. Give me an opportunity to change your mind."

"Jeffrey, I…" She couldn't find words to refute the pleading in his eyes.

"A week. Only a week. I ask nothing more."

Her stomach fluttering at the lie, she said softly, "A week."

"That's all I ask." He bent forward to kiss her cheek before leaving the room.

****

"Biggs, I cannot tell you how much this means to me." Lottie sat beside him on the wagon seat as they drove through the night toward the coast.

"It's the least I can do for a fellow countryman… woman," he said gruffly.

"But if Sir Jeffrey discovers you've aided me in my escape…"

"There's slight chance of that. I am the head groom. None of the lads who work for me are likely to say I've taken a horse and wagon out for a midnight drive."

"But will you be back in time in the morning before you're missed?"

"I've told the lads to inform Sir Jeffrey that I've taken this old mare into the village to the blacksmith's to have her hooves looked to. He's not an early riser. He'll suspect nothing."

Feeling better about Biggs's involvement in her escape, she settled back on the seat. She knew he wouldn't be implicated in the theft she'd perpetrated on Sir Jeffrey's desk. She'd left a note accepting full culpability. And she'd taken only what she'd felt she would need to pay her passage on a ship to America. Once she was settled in the new country and had obtained gainful employment, she planned to reimburse him both for the funds and the cost of the clothing she'd taken.

"I'll be missin' ya, mistress," Biggs said. "And I know for certain sure Beauty will as well."

"I shall miss both of you, as well," she said. "But I must go. There are things in my past that could make life difficult for Sir Jeffrey."

"Not a Jacobite, were ya?"

"Let's just say I sympathize."

"Aye, well, good for you, lass. If I'd thought the cause had a snowball's chance in hell, I'd have gone back to fight after I got out of prison."

"You were in prison?"

"Oh, aye. I was a rebel once, but no more. Too old to run the hills or ride like the wind. But my best wishes to those who continue the fight."

Content in Biggs's reliability, she settled back to plan her future as they lurched along toward the coast.

****

She was standing in line waiting on the wharf to be transported out to the ship resting at anchor offshore when his voice startled her.

"Charlotte."

Whirling, she saw Sir Jeffrey striding toward her, more disheveled than she'd ever seen him, mud spattered on his breeches and boots, his jacket rumpled, his face pale and tense.

"Jeffrey, how did you find me?" The question was a gasp.

"I went out to the stable to check on one of the mares early this morning. She'd seemed a tad unwell. I caught Biggs returning with a wagon and a weary horse. Suspicious of his tale, I checked on you and found you gone.

"With threats more dire than anything I've ever uttered in my life, I confronted Biggs. He eventually confessed that he'd driven you here. He also said it was too late for me to stop you...that, by this time, your ship had already sailed. I determined to prove him wrong and rode my swiftest horse nearly into the ground to get here in time, and I did." He took a deep breath. "You promised me a week...a week in which I might change your mind." The words carried a begging desperation that tore at her heart.

"I know, Jeffrey, but I have to get away...before your association with me destroys you."

"I don't believe you. What can you have done that could possibly lead to such dire consequences?"

"Please don't ask. Just let me go and understand it's for the best...for both of us."

"And how do you propose to survive in America? I understand it's still largely a wilderness, no fit place for a woman alone."

"I have a friend, a very good friend. He'll see me settled."

"You have strong reasons to believe this friend will

protect you? Charlotte, can you be certain?"

"Yes, I can. Douglas and I have a history of looking out for each other, as a brother and sister would. He will continue to do so, I've no doubt."

"Charlotte, Charlotte…" He heaved a great sigh. "Is there nothing I can do that will convince you to stay?"

"No, there isn't. Jeffrey, please believe me when I say my leaving is best for both of us." She raised on her toes to plant a kiss on his cheek. "I love you, Sir Jeffrey. No one could have been kinder or more understanding to me. I simply don't feel toward you as I should if I were to accept your generous offer of marriage."

"Then, at least, accept this." He reached into his waistcoat and pulled out a small cloth bag that jingled. "It will help defer any expenses you may encounter."

"Jeffrey…" Shamed, she felt it thrust into her hand. "I cannot accept…"

"Yes, you can."

"There is something I must tell you." Aching with humiliation, she looked up into his eyes, the pouch of gold heavy in her hand. "I stole from the desk in your office. That is how I've been able to pay for my passage. I plan to return it to you as soon as I find gainful employment in New Brunswick."

"A paltry sum, I'm sure." He shrugged. "You've more than repaid me with your companionship these past weeks. I'd give all that was in my safe and the bulk of my estate if I could convince you to stay."

"Jeffrey…" She reached up to put her gloved hand against his cheek, too moved to say more.

"Your luggage is aboard, miss. You'd best move

along. The last longboat is about to shove off for the vessel."

"Yes, yes, of course," she replied, giving Sir Jeffrey Tinsdale a last, long, loving look before she followed the big, burly man to the end of the quay and eased herself down the ladder into the longboat.

As the sailors bent to the oars and the vessel headed out toward the waiting ship, she looked back toward shore to see him standing on the wharf, watching her go. She raised a gloved hand in farewell as his image was swallowed up by incoming fog.

It was the end of safety and fine living conditions. Her stomach roiling, she swallowed hard and tried to settle her fluttering innards. She had no idea what lay ahead. She only knew leaving the British Isles and Sir Jeffrey Tinsdale had been her only choice.

Chapter Nine

Jack Wallace pushed the last of their belongings into the back of the farm wagon. He covered the collection of boxes and trunks with a sheet of sailcloth and secured it in place with a length of rope. With a deft move, he cut off the excess with a long-bladed hunting knife and pushed the weapon into its scabbard at his belt.

The movement had been reflective. It brought a rueful grimace to his face. He hadn't felt the need to carry a weapon in years. Still, he and his young daughter were heading into rough territory with wild animals and maybe even footpads or highwaymen. Even though he strongly denounced violence, he knew it was sometimes necessary to defend loved ones.

He rolled stiff shoulders. He wasn't young anymore. Nor exactly old, but it had been years since he'd been forced to fight. Would he be able to put up an effective defense if the need arose?

As he stepped back to survey his family caravan, another thought assailed him, and a sardonic grin curled the corners of his mouth. With an old mare pulling a decrepit farm wagon, it hardly looked tempting to robbers.

In his mind the wagon had only one container of value. It was the box that held his books and papers. He'd taken special care in packing them. Now he wondered why he'd bothered. What good would they be to him? Certainly they'd be of no value to robbers.

"Here she is, Papa." Interrupting his thought, his daughter came out of the stable leading the donkey. "All brushed and fed and ready for adventure." She smiled at her father as she handed him the little animal's lead rope.

"Good." He took the tether from her hand and secured it to the back of the wagon. "Cathy, I hope you'll enjoy living in Riverhaven...you and Grace."

"Of course we will, Papa." She favored him with a bright smile before turning toward the front of the wagon. "Do you think Glory will be able to manage?" Lines of concern crinkling her face, she glanced back at her father as she paused to rub the mare's graying snout. "She's not young anymore."

"She'll manage." Hoping he sounded more confident than he felt, he joined her. "When we get to Riverhaven, we can retire her to fine pastures and a warm barn. Now get aboard. We have to be on our way."

She climbed to the seat and waited for him to join her. He shook the reins over the mare's back, and she started off at a plodding walk. As they drove away from the manse in the gray dawning of a misty spring morning, he glanced over at her. Wearing a woolen cap and cape, her hands in thick gloves, she sat up proudly on the seat of the old farm wagon.

She'd asked no questions about their early hour of departure, although he guessed she knew the reason. Better to leave before most of the town was awake, before anyone could toss more insults or, God forbid, rocks at them.

"Get along there, Glory." He urged the mare to a slow trot as they reached the outskirts of Fredericton. "We've a long road ahead of us."

"It will be fine, Papa." She touched his arm and smiled up at him. "An adventure."

"Yes," he said softly. "An adventure."

****

He glanced at his daughter sitting beside him on the wagon seat. Although she remained holding herself stiffly upright, by casting furtive looks in her direction, he'd seen her shoulders slump from time to time. It had been a long, slow, cold, and wearying drive from Fredericton. They'd had to camp overnight and now it was growing late in the second day.

He'd reckoned that they should be in Riverhaven before dark, but he wouldn't press the old mare pulling the wagon, his daughter, or the donkey to reach their destination. If they had to spend another night camped by the roadside rather than exhaust his small caravan, he'd do it. He drew off to the side of the trail.

"Whoa," he called.

The mare stopped and blew. She was weary.

"Why are we stopping, Papa?" His daughter came quickly alert. "Are we very near Riverhaven?"

"Quite near, but I see a clearing with a brook over to our left. Our beasts could stand some refreshment...as could I."

Carefully he directed the horse down the slight incline into the meadow. Once there, he wound the reins around the whip stand and jumped to the ground. Before he could help her alight, his daughter had joined him and was hurrying to the rear of the wagon to untie her donkey.

"She must be thirsty," she said, leading the little animal toward the water.

"Be careful," he called after her as he began to release the mare from the wagon. "Not too much at once."

He was involved in freeing Glory from the traces when he heard her scream and the donkey's frantic braying. Swinging from his task, he saw a large wildcat had leaped onto the little animal's back. Screaming its triumph, it pulled Grace down. His daughter, thrown aside by the attack, lay on the ground.

Heart pounding a mad tattoo at the back of his throat, he wrenched his knife from its scabbard at his belt and raced toward the horror.

The next moments were a tangled nightmare. Later, he barely remembered the sequence. All he recalled was that he managed to pull the cat from the donkey by plunging his knife deep somewhere into its body. He and the cat rolled to the ground together. The beast rebounded to its feet with lightning speed and crouched for an attack on Jack as he struggled up on an elbow.

With a roar that echoed through the forest, the creature sprang. It was in midair when the shot rang out. In a nightmare vision, Jack watched it crumple to the ground, blood spurting from its head. It convulsed for a moment before lying still.

Chapter Ten

"Aire you all right, laddie?" A voice thick with Highland accent inquired.

Turning, Jack saw a tall, broad-shouldered man looming over him, his face crinkled with concern. A smoking pistol hung from his hand.

"Aye." Through a haze of shock, he saw Cathy, her arms about the donkey's neck as both struggled to their feet. Blood flowed from several wounds on the little animal's hindquarters. But, praise God, his daughter appeared unharmed.

As his mind cleared, he saw a second wagon, pulled by a team of drays, easing down the slight slope from the road to join them in the clearing. Leaving a young boy holding the reins, a woman jumped down from the driver's seat and ran toward his daughter and her pet.

"Child, are you all right?" The woman put an arm about Cathy's shoulders.

"Yes...yes...but Papa..." Cathy cast a glance over at her father still on the ground.

"I'm well, Cathy, just a bit winded." Jack tried to sound calm as their rescuer held down a big hand to help him to his feet. "Not to worry."

"Grace is injured, terribly injured." Her face was deathly white, her eyes mirroring her distress as she turned back to her little animal.

"We'll tend to her," the woman said gently. She was already examining the gashes.

"Quite the scare you got, I reckon." The man holding the pistol stepped back to look down at the dead cat. "A cougar. Not many around here, but enough to keep a lad on his toes when traveling through the woods."

"Thank you." Jack found his voice.

"Just glad we happened to be passin'." He dismissed gratitude.

"Brodie, get that jar of honey from the wagon...and the bottle of laudanum." The woman barely turned to her companion as she spoke, keeping her attention on the donkey.

Jack, in spite of the horror of the recent attack, was surprised as he got his first good look at her. She was one of the most beautiful women he'd ever seen. A face of angelic likeness, surrounded by a froth of titian curls, glanced over at the men.

"Aye, aye, lass." Stuffing the pistol into his belt, the man she'd called Brodie loped off to do her bidding.

"Now you stay put, young Alex," he ordered the child on its seat. "Your mother has work to do. Mind your sister. She mustn't be left alone."

"Aye, Papa."

****

In the ensuing minutes, Jack Wallace watched as Brodie held the donkey while the woman poured brown liquid down its throat, then proceeded to douse the hemorrhaging wound with honey.

Shortly the trembling animal grew quiet.

"No!" The cry came from Cathy as Grace closed her eyes and wobbled on her hooves.

"She's not dying, my dear." The woman, her hands still bloody from treating the wounds, favored her with a reassuring smile. "I simply gave her something to make her sleep and stay out of pain for a time."

"Yes?"

"Yes."

"I'm Brodie MacMillan." The man who'd shot the big cat held out a hand to Jack as the girl and woman continued to stand beside the little animal. "The lady is my wife, Louisa. She's by way of being a fine healer. Yonder in the wagon is our son, Alex, and in a wee bed in the back is our daughter, Ceilidh."

"Jack Wallace." Jack accepted the gesture.

Brodie MacMillan. Surely this couldn't be the same man whose reputation had been the bane of redcoats in the Highlands years ago.

"Wallace, you say? Well, now." The other man's expression combined astonishment and amazement.

"The young lady is my daughter, Catherine... Cathy." His thoughts jumped back to more immediate matters as he saw blood running between his fingers.

"Good to meet you, Jack Wallace." Brodie MacMillan's expression returned to mobility. "Hie there, laddie, you're hurt."

"Gentlemen, we need your assistance immediately," the woman ordered as the donkey swayed on its hooves. "The laudanum is making her sleepy. She mustn't be allowed to fall. Help us ease her down."

The two men hurried forward and helped the women to lower the swaying animal gently to the ground.

"Papa, what are we going to do?" Cathy looked up

at her father once the animal was lying on the ground. "We can't leave Grace here, and we have no space in our wagon to carry her."

"Dunnae greet, lassie." As his companion spoke, Jack heard the deep Highland tones with which he'd once been familiar. "She'll be fine. My wife is the best healer in miles. We'll make room to transport her in our wagon. But," he continued as he knelt by the donkey, "first, let my wife see to your hand, Jack Wallace. It's bleedin' a fair bit."

"Yes." Louisa MacMillan went to examine Jack's hand. "Brodie, I need a bandage."

"Oh, aye."

The man pulled off his coat and, with a quick wrench, tore the sleeve from his shirt. "Here you go, lass," he said handing it to his wife.

A most unusual couple, but thank God we encountered them.

"Come along, Mr. Wallace," she instructed, heading for the stream. "We must wash that wound."

In very short time, she'd cleaned the cut expertly, applied honey, and wrapped it securely in her husband's shirtsleeve.

Brodie MacMillan, seeing it was done, strode to his conveyance and began to gather sacks from its cargo space. "Will you give me a hand, Jack Wallace?" he continued as he carried bundles toward the other wagon. "We'll empty our cargo into your conveyance and make space for the wee beast."

"Yes, we will." His wife had gone quickly to the stream, washed her hands, and was returning, ready to help again.

She vaulted easily into the back of their wagon,

gathered up a bundle, and thrust it into her son's arms. "Alex MacMillan, I'm entrusting you with your sister," she said.

"Aye, Mama." The child made no protest but looked at his mother with serious blue eyes.

She jumped to the ground and returned to the group about the donkey. "Do you have a sturdy blanket, Mr. Wallace?" she asked. "If you do, we can slide it under the donkey. With all of us lifting together, we can get her into our wagon."

"I have better." He began to rummage through his belongings. "I have a bit of sailcloth. I thought it might come in handy as a tent on the journey…which it did."

"Guid, very guid." Brodie caught the rough canvas Jack tossed to him.

When she'd finished, with all lifting together, they managed to get the donkey into the back of the MacMillan wagon.

"Now we'd best be gettin' under way." Brodie MacMillan turned to him. "I'll be leadin' the way drivin' your wagon. Your hand isn't up to holdin' reins."

"But yours…" Jack Wallace indicated the team of Percherons harnessed to it.

"My wife is more than capable of handlin' a team," he replied as he took Louisa's arm to help her aboard. "Come along, lass." He turned to Cathy. "I'd be right obliged if you'd ride with my wife and children. She could do with someone to hold our wee daughter."

"But you don't know where we're going." Jack Wallace looked up at his companion as the man climbed aboard his wagon. Although Brodie MacMillan was apparently a man accustomed to taking charge,

Jack couldn't remain passive as to their destination.

"Climb up here beside me and dunnae greet. It's growin' dark and promises to be a frosty night. You're comin' to our home where there's a good barn and feed for your beasts and where Louisa left a pot of stew ready to heat up on the fire. Tonight, while you and the donkey need tendin', you'll stay with us."

"I thank you most kindly, but we're bound for the village manse. I'd be obliged if you'd direct us there. I've been sent to take charge of the church in Riverhaven. I understand your minister has gone off to Scotland with his family for a visit to his parents."

"You're a reverend?" As Jack joined him on the seat, Brodie swung fully to face him. "Bloody hell…ah, excuse me, Reverend. Well, now."

His mouth curling in a sardonic grin, he turned back to the task at hand and clucked to the mare. When she hesitated, Jack advised, "Her name is Glory. She's accustomed to being called such. At the moment, she's more than a tad weary. She's pulled this wagon all the way from Fredericton."

"A fine name. Get along with you, Glory lass, not much farther." He hesitated before continuing, "Your wife will be comin' along shortly?"

"I'm a widower." Jack avoided his companion's questioning glance. "My wife died several years ago."

"Life is not always fair, is it?"

"Indeed it is not always what we hope and plan."

"Aye, aye." Brodie MacMillan's acknowledgement came out gruffly, leading Jack to suspect he, too, had suffered loss and understood.

As they headed down the trail, Jack stole a furtive glance at his companion. The more he had a chance to peruse him, the more he became convinced he knew who he was. But alive and here?

"You're starin', laddie." A sly grin curling his lips, Brodie cast him a furtive glance as the mare moved down the trail at a sedate walk. "You're thinkin' we might have met afore...maybe in the Highlands?"

"Aye." He dropped into the accent he'd suppressed for so many years. "I'm thinkin' you were a friend of my brother."

"And who might that brother be?" Jack caught a mischievous twinkle in his companion's eyes.

"Hamish Wallace...better known as the outlaw Highland Harry."

"Ah, I thought there was a familiarity about you, laddie." Brodie was all-out grinning. "We met only once, when Hamish risked goin' home for supplies... when we were blessed-near starvin' after the redcoats had all but run us to death. I thought you had the look of him about you."

"And you would be Brazen Brodie, his outlaw companion. I never did hear your surname. We thought you were dead...both of you."

"Right sad for the English, but no. We're both hale and hearty."

"What? How can you know about Hamish?"

"Because we both live near here. We share a millin' business. We're respectable as hell now— excuse me once again—outlaws no more, at least not Hamish."

"Hamish is here, in this community?" Astonished, Jack stared at the man beside him on the seat.

"Aye, aye, a fair upstandin' member of the district." He chuckled. "Married with a bonny wife, seven stepchildren, and two of his own blood." There was a pause before Brodie MacMillan, glancing over at him, continued, "I'm reckonin' this news took the wind out of your sails for a minute."

"Aye." An array of memories was dashing through Jack's mind about the brother he'd believed dead—memories of their childhood, of their dispute on how best to deal with the English, their bitter parting.

"You'll be wantin' to see him. I'll tell him you've arrived."

"I do want to see him." Jack drew a deep breath. "But whether he'll want to see me is another question. We didn't part on the best of terms."

"Aye, I ken." Brodie adjusted the reins in his hands and grew serious. "We were all out for fightin' and you thought there were better ways to settle the troubles, as I recall."

"You were freedom fighters," Jack said. "Sadly, my peaceful methods didn't have much effect. Our people are still being abused by the English, perhaps even more so now they're seriously clearing the land for sheep."

"We should go back—all of us—and beat the arses off the bastards!" Brodie's expression hardened.

"You couldn't win. It would be Culloden all over again—pikes and axes against muskets and cannons."

"Aye, aye, you're right." Weariness filled his words, but then his tone picked up. "Still, I'd like a chance to beat them off our land once and for all. Get along there, Glory. The manse is but a short distance ahead."

Chapter Eleven

Jack got his first introduction to his new home through the gathering dusk. Brodie had turned off the main trail up a lane that led to a small, neat, gabled farmhouse, its whitewashed façade welcoming in the gloom. Behind it he could see a decent-sized barn outlined in the darkness.

"There's a right nice bit of cultivated land out back," Brodie said as he halted the weary mare before the veranda. "Lachlan and Iona were good farmers."

"Lachlan?" Jack turned to his companion. "I understood my predecessor was Edward Morgan."

"Oh, aye, that's what he chose to call himself after he fled Scotland...afraid they might come after him and his wife, who was with child at the time." He swung down from the wagon. "In the Old Country he was Lachlan Cameron and his wife Iona, when he rode with Harry and me. When he came to Riverhaven, he changed his name to Edward Morgan and his wife's to Mary. Now, let's move along. There're fires to light and animals to stable. This old lady"—he slapped the mare on the rump—"is about tuckered."

"But where's the church?" Jack got down to join him as the second wagon drew up behind them.

"Out on a bit of an island beyond." Brodie indicated a lane leading off to the right. "A fine spot, pretty as a picture. The first clergyman who built this place decided to keep body and spirit apart...that is, farm and church. I think he made a good decision. Louisa," he called out to his wife, "drive on to the stable. Jack and I will be there in a shake of a lamb's tail to help you with the donkey."

As he spoke, he'd been freeing Glory from the traces. Leading the exhausted mare, he turned her to follow the other wagon beyond the house.

Jack drew a deep breath before following. If everyone in Riverhaven were like the MacMillans, he and Cathy might have a fine life in the community.

****

Jack awoke the following morning and stretched. It took a moment to realize he was in a bedroom in the Riverhaven manse, that he and Cathy had arrived there in a cold, rainy dusk the previous evening and, aided by Brodie MacMillan and his family, managed to begin to settle in. He stretched again and sat up.

Sunlight beamed in through the lace curtains on the window. The previous minister's wife had been a fine housekeeper. From what he'd been able to gather the previous night, the entire small house showed evidence of having been well maintained, as had the stable and grounds. Even the double bed in which he'd spent the night had been neatly made up with fresh linen and warm quilts.

Double bed. He heaved a sigh. It had been a long time since he'd had need of a bed for two. He missed Helen. They might not have been passionately in love, but they'd been comfortable together, respectful of each other, and Helen of being the dutiful clergyman's wife. And she'd given him Cathy.

He thought of Brodie MacMillan and his amazing,

beautiful wife. What would it be like to be married to such a woman?

With a grunt, he moved to leave the bed and discovered muscles that ached from the journey followed by the fight with the big cat. His brother had been right. He wasn't much of a fighting man.

And now he'd rediscovered Hamish...or Harry, as he was now known. What would be the result of their meeting again? With an effort, he pulled himself to his feet and began to dress. Best to put that concern aside. He and Cathy had much settling in to do.

"Papa, come and see!" He'd finished pulling on breeches and shirt when Cathy's voice summoned him from the bedroom across the hall.

"Look!" she exclaimed when he joined her. Standing by a window in a floor-length nightshift, she spread an arm to indicate a fenced pasture, at the rear of the house, brightening with spring greenery. "Isn't it wonderful! Won't Glory and Grace have a wonderful time out there?"

"They certainly will." He put an arm loosely about her shoulders. "Cathy, I hope you'll be happy here."

"I will, Papa. I know I will." She turned back to the bed with her clothing hanging over its end. "Now if you'll go downstairs and get the fire started, I'll be there directly to see to your breakfast...after I take a quick run out to the barn and check on Grace."

"Cathy, I don't want you to become my servant." He looked after her, frowning. "As soon as we're settled in, I'll find a housekeeper."

"Perhaps one just a tad better than Mrs. Keen?" She cast him a mischievous glance.

"Aye, one chust a tad better than Mrs. Keen." He

let a grin curl his mouth.

"I do so enjoy it when you let your Highland accent come through." Her eyes sparkled as she looked at him.

"Well, perhaps now you'll be hearing a lot more of it, here in Riverhaven where I'm guessing it's not to my advantage to hide it. Now we'd best be getting on with the day. I believe a visit to the village is in order. We need supplies, and it will give us a chance to meet some of the residents."

He left the room and made his way down to the small, neat kitchen, wondering where on earth he'd find anyone willing to work for the meagre stipend that was all he could afford.

****

Jack halted Glory on the crest of the low hill. The mare, restored by feed, water, and a night's rest, was once again pulling the wagon as best her advanced age would allow.

Below, the village of Riverhaven lay basking in spring sunlight on the bank of a wide river. Consisting of several buildings, some log, some clapboard, it had a single, muddy road running between them. People were moving along it, ladies with baskets, men in working garb.

About a quarter mile down river, three ocean-going vessels in various stages of construction rested in dry docks. Beyond these structures, the river glistened in the sunlight, small waves crinkling its surface.

"Oh, Papa, it's so pretty...pretty and rustic." Beside him on the wagon seat his daughter was enthusiastic, her face bright.

"Don't you mean pretty rustic?" He grinned over at

her. "It's a far cry from Fredericton."

"That's just fine with me." She tossed her head defiantly. "I was getting deathly weary of that place."

"Very well then." He shook the reins over Glory's back to start her moving down the incline. "Let's go into this pretty village and see what it has to offer."

At the beginning of the street, Cathy pointed to a sturdy building.

"What is that, Papa?" she asked. A sign that read "Magistrate" hung over the door.

"I assume that's the office of the local peacekeeper and general community factotum," he said. "A village this small could hardly warrant a full slate of officials as Fredericton does. Whoever this man is, he's probably in charge of most activities that take place in Riverhaven."

They reached the center of the village. Jack drew Glory up to a hitching rail in front of a building with the sign "Angus Harris, General Merchant" over its door.

"I believe this is the place we're seeking," he said. He climbed down and reached up to help his daughter to the ground, but she jumped on her own.

"You mustn't make a baby of me, Papa." She grinned at him. "I'm a frontier woman now."

"Not exactly," he replied as he tied Glory to the hitching rail. "But I know you can fend for yourself…in most situations."

They entered the store together, and both took a moment to stare about at the wide array of items offered. Food, along with farm and carpentry equipment, filled the front of the shop. Toward the rear were shelves stocked with rolls of cloth, blankets, and household utensils.

"Good morning to you, sir and young lady." The big man behind the counter favored them with a wide smile on his broad face. "I'm guessing you're our new reverend and his daughter. Brodie MacMillan was just in and said he'd met you on the road yesterday."

"That's correct." Jack strode forward and offered his bandaged hand. "Jack Wallace, and this is my daughter, Catherine…Cathy."

"Angus Harris, at your service. You've been injured?"

"Aye, a small accident. So Brodie MacMillan has already been here to inform you of our arrival." Jack knew the news travelled quickly in small communities, but this was amazing.

"Aye, the lad gets around."

"Did he also tell you he saved my daughter and her donkey from a cougar?"

"Never mentioned it, Reverend, but I'm delighted to hear it. Brodie is a brave lad and never one to brag about his deeds. Oh, by the way"—he waved a hand to indicate a young man who'd been involved in examining a length of chain near the rear of the store— "this is Brodie's nephew…unofficial nephew…Geordie Fowler. His stepfather is Harry Wallace."

"A pleasure to meet you, Reverend." The lad came forward, hand extended to greet Jack. "And you as well, Miss Wallace. Uncle Brodie told us as how you'd arrived." He bowed to Cathy.

With a start, Jack saw interest sparkle in his daughter's blue eyes as she dipped a curtsy to the handsome, broad-shouldered young fellow. He'd known Cathy was getting to the age, but still—not with this lad. Not with his brother's son…stepson.

"Mr. Fowler." She cast him a demure smile.

"I have a list." To divert himself from thoughts of his daughter maturing, Jack thrust a piece of paper toward the shopkeeper.

"Well, then, let us get right to it." The shopkeeper frowned as he read down the list. "Ah, now here there's a problem, Reverend. Seed potatoes. I had precious few and they've all been sold. Most of the farmers hereabouts keep enough from their previous year's crops for planting. Maybe if you check the root cellar at the manse you'll be able to scare up enough for a crop. Geordie?" He turned to the young man who stood smiling steadily at Cathy. "I'll just be putting those chains on the company's account, will I?"

"Aye, aye." Geordie Fowler's attention was riveted on Cathy as he replied absently.

The Scottish inflection in the lad's speech did nothing to reassure Jack, knowing how susceptible his daughter was to it.

"Good day to you, Reverend, Miss Cathy." Geordie Fowler touched his forelock, smiled a smile Jack saw as directed at his daughter, and walked out of the store.

Cathy stared after him, her lips curling at the corners.

****

During the course of their visit to the village, Jack and his daughter had the opportunity to meet a number of residents, and while Jack gathered they were each taking his measure, he sensed no hostility among them. They'd liked Reverend Edward Morgan, he came to understand, but weren't unwilling to give this new man a chance. He could handle that attitude, he decided as they drove out of the village later in the morning.

"He's quite handsome, isn't he, Papa?" Cathy broke in on his thoughts as they turned into the manse driveway.

"Who?" He couldn't resist pretending he didn't understand.

"Geordie Fowler, of course. Oh, Papa, don't tease."

"And you behave yourself, young lady. You only just met the lad. He may be the village lothario," he teased.

"I seriously doubt it." She jumped down as he halted Glory in front of the manse. "His smile is much too shy. Now I must see to Grace. I'm sure she's been missing me."

As she ran off toward the pasture, Jack watched her go. With a rueful smirk, he eased himself to the ground and went to the rear of the wagon to unload their purchases. His daughter was growing up, noticing young men. He knew it was normal, but he wished she had a woman's guidance at this stage of her life.

He wondered about this young Fowler chap. Harry Wallace's stepson, the shopkeeper had said. That much had been obvious. Harry hadn't been in this country long enough to have fathered a lad of that age. Not blood. Still, raised by his rebel brother… He could only hope Cathy wasn't too enamored with the lad.

****

Late in the afternoon, Jack had further reason for concern when Geordie Fowler rode up in front of the manse on a fine black gelding. Sitting on the veranda, having finished taking the measure of the farm land and doing barn work, Jack was taking a brief respite before supper.

"Good afternoon, sir." Geordie was respectful. "I heard you needed seed potatoes. I've brought you a few." He indicated a burlap sack tied to his saddle.

"That's very kind of you, Mr. Fowler." Jack stood and walked out to accept the offering. "I did find a few in the root cellar, as Mr. Harris suggested, but not so many as I'd hoped to plant." He looked up at the handsome young lad. "Will you step down and take a rest?"

At that moment, Cathy appeared in the doorway. She was wearing an apron, her face flushed from making supper at the hearth.

"Mr. Fowler, hello." She bobbed a curtsy and smiled.

"Miss Wallace." He doffed his cap, and Jack saw a look he'd seen before on many a young male face.

Smitten with my daughter, he is.

"Mr. Fowler has brought us some seed potatoes," he said.

"That's very kind of you, Mr. Fowler." She advanced to the edge of the veranda. "We're about to have supper. Will you join us?"

"Most kind of you, miss, but I must be getting home. Mother makes a head count at the meal, what with there being so many of us. She has to reassure herself we're all there." His grin was shy but sufficiently mischievous to catch a young woman's fancy. He leaned to drop the sack into Jack's waiting hands and then swung his mount about as Jack stepped back to the veranda. "And by the way, everyone calls me Geordie." He put his heels to the horse's sides and set off at a full gallop.

"I'll put these around back," Jack said as his

daughter gazed after the young man's retreating figure. "And, you, young lady, best be checking on our supper."

"Aye, Papa." Her tone was teasing as she skipped back into the house.

Chapter Twelve

"Hello, the house!" Brodie MacMillan's shout startled Cathy and Jack as they were finishing their noon meal the following day.

"Mr. MacMillan." Enthusiastically, Cathy was on her feet and heading for the door. "Perhaps Mrs. MacMillan and the children are with him, come to visit. How lovely!"

When Jack reached the front door shortly after his daughter, he saw only the man himself, mounted on the red mare, with a chestnut horse at the end of a lead rope behind him.

"You wouldn't be doin' me a small favor, would you, Reverend?" Affable grin in place, he greeted the minister.

"Of course, if I can, Mr. MacMillan. What might that be?"

"This little gelding." He indicated the dark brown animal. "He's too small for mill work. He's the result of an accidental breeding between one of our drays and a saddle mare and not good enough for the work of either his sire or his dam. For certain sure, he's not worth his feed at our operations. I don't want to see him put down—he's a right kind and willin' lad—but unless I can find a home for him…"

Cathy ran down the steps and began to rub the chestnut's snout. "Oh, Papa, just look! He likes me.

Can we take him…please?"

"Well…" Jack hesitated, strongly suspecting Brodie MacMillan was telling a bit of a tale in order to provide him with a decent horse.

"He's fine under both saddle and harness, and gentle as a lamb." Brodie watched the girl fondling the horse. "You can use him in the fields or for ridin'. And," he added slyly, "you can give that old beast of yours a well-deserved retirement."

"We do need a younger horse, Papa." Cathy's eyes pleaded with him in a way he was seldom able to resist. "And, as Mr. MacMillan, says, Glory needs her rest."

"Very well." He'd put Glory before plow the previous day. She'd stumbled so severely he'd unharnessed her and turned her out to graze.

"Thank you, thank you, Papa." Cathy brimmed over with happiness as Brodie handed her the lead rope. "I'll take him to the pasture that he might meet Glory and Grace. Thank you, Mr. MacMillan, a hundred thousand thanks. Oh, look at his face, that white streak. I'll call him Blaze…that is, if I may…unless he has another name."

"You can name him as you choose, lass." Brodie grinned. "We never did get around to callin' him anything more than 'whoa' and 'walk on.' "

"I will be paying you for the animal." Jack spoke once his daughter had led the gelding away. "I cannot accept such a fine animal as a gift."

"Of course you will pay for him." Brodie grinned down at him. "In her feed and care. I didn't want to see the little beast destroyed, but at the mill and farm we can't go havin' pets. Givin' him a decent home will be payment enough."

He touched his hat brim, swung his mount about, and galloped off down the lane.

An outlaw with a heart of gold. The analogy flashed across Jack's mind as he watched him go.

****

Jack returned alone to the altar of the small whitewashed church on the island after his congregation had departed. Drawing a deep breath, he paused for a moment to look out over the empty benches that earlier had been crowded with villagers. While he guessed many of them had come simply out of curiosity to see their new minister and discover what he had to offer, he hoped he'd impressed them sufficiently to inspire their return. He turned his back and began to organize the few books and papers he'd left on a small desk.

"Well, brother, we meet again."

The voice, familiar even after years, made him jerk about to see a tall, dark-haired man standing at the back of the church, feet parted shoulder width, hands on narrow hips.

"Hamish." He managed to sound calm and in control. "I didn't see you at service this morning. I did have the pleasure of meeting your wife and children. A fine, large family."

"Aye, well, I thought it best we have our first meeting alone." He walked confidently up the aisle, booted footsteps ringing over the board floor.

"A wise move." Jack gathered the mixture of emotions moving about in his gut and came down to meet his brother as he stopped half way up the aisle. "It's good to see you, Hamish." He held out his hand.

"Is it?" His brother ignored the offer. "You had

harsh words for me the last time we met...and parted. Words to the effect that he who lives by the sword will die by it."

"I still believe violence is no answer." Jack let his unaccepted hand drop back to his side.

"And I still believe that sometimes there is no other way."

The two men faced each other in the silence of the sanctuary, both holding to the beliefs that had separated them years earlier in the Highlands. It was Harry who finally spoke.

"I thought possibly you'd changed your view. Brodie told me how you attacked that cougar. He said you were holding your own against the beast before he arrived."

"The creature had attacked my daughter's donkey. My child would have been next."

"So you'd fight to save your bairn, but not your other family members back in the Highlands? That's a bit of a double standard, isn't it, *Reverend*?"

"Immediate danger takes precedence over starting a battle...a battle with no hope of winning. I'd hoped that here, in this new country, you'd found a better way, a peaceful way," Jack said.

"Mostly, but when the need arises, I'm still capable of putting up a scrap."

"Hamish, I think it's time we put old feuds behind us." Jack drew a deep breath. "We can start afresh here. Come outside—I'd like you to meet my daughter. She'll be waiting for me. I know she'd welcome meeting her uncle."

"I'm sure she's a fine lass, but I've no desire to renew our brotherly status, Jack. You refused to come wi' Brodie and me to fight those English bastards. You were willin' to let innocent women and children, even our own family, be run off their lands into the snow. I canna forgive your actions. I came here today only to let you know how things stand between us...how nothin' has changed. Oh, and by the way, chust a word of warnin'." He paused on his way to the door and swung back. "My business partner and long-time companion may have helped you out of a bad situation with that cat and given you one of his cast-off geldin's, but be forewarned. While Brodie is a guid lad, none better to have a man's back in a fight, he's remained what he was in the Highlands...a law unto himself. He'll fight for what he sees as right no matter how those in authority view the situation. A guid lad who'll give you the shirt right off his back when the need arises, Brodie MacMillan can nevertheless drag those around him into one of his scrapes without a moment's forethought. So have a care around him."

He turned and strode out of the church.

A wry grin quirked Jack's lips. No matter what his brother said, he couldn't help believing Brodie MacMillan was a good man. And if he hadn't already given him the shirt off his back, he'd at least given Jack the sleeve from it.

"Papa?" His daughter interrupted his thoughts as she came back into the church. "Whoever was that man who just left? He was striding away as if the devil were after him."

"Your uncle," he said ruefully. "That, child, was your Uncle Harry."

****

Jack leaned back in the chair in the manse's small

study and closed his eyes. The heat of the early summer day had wearied him more than the work he'd done, planting in the fields. He had to admit it. He was aging, more fit for a position in Fredericton at the University.

A slight sound outside made him jerk alert. Looking out the window, he saw Cathy standing beside Grace and next to them a young man he recognized, holding the reins of a coal black horse. Cathy was smiling as Geordie Fowler petted the donkey.

Memories of his own early relationship with a pretty lass in the Highlands invaded his thoughts. She'd been about the same age as Cathy, he a couple of years older. She'd been lovely, the most beautiful creature he could have imagined. She'd been romantic, all flowers and poetry, and he'd struggled to keep their meetings on an ethereal, platonic level. But he'd been young and full of spirit and…he had to admit not without lustful longings.

He'd become too passionate in their love-making. Shocked and startled, she'd rejected him and fled. Ashamed of his actions, he'd let some time pass before he'd dared to allow himself into another relationship with a young woman.

Apprehension rose in his gut. This handsome young lad was about the same age as he'd been when he'd made his first unfortunate attempt at physical love. He could only assume Geordie Fowler was possessed of similar urges.

Furthermore, he struggled to find more immediate reasons to be apprehensive. With his brother vehemently opposed to any friendship between their families, was it wise for Harry's stepson to be getting involved with his daughter? At any rate, she was far too young to be meeting alone with a young man.

He stood, squared his shoulders, and headed outside.

"Good afternoon, Mr. Fowler," he used a formal address to greet the lad.

"Good afternoon, sir." Geordie Fowlie fingered the cap he held in his hands as he turned to face him. He had the good grace to look a bit sheepish. "I was on my way into the village and thought I'd drop in to see if there was anything I might get for you."

"Thank you, no. My daughter and I are well supplied." Fighting down his parental instincts, he took on the role of affable clergyman. "I trust your family is well?"

"Very well. My mother was wondering if she might send along a bit of bread starter that you might make your own bread."

"That would be welcome." Cathy was quick to step into the conversation. "We would enjoy having fresh bread, wouldn't we, Papa?"

"Yes…yes, of course." Jack stumbled the affirmative response even as he guessed this was simply the young man's excuse to visit again.

"Then I'll bring some by tomorrow." Geordie Fowler gathered up his reins and swung back onto the black gelding. "I'll bid you good day."

He paused for a moment to favor Cathy with a devil-may-care smile before turning the horse about and bounding it off down the trail to the village road.

"He's very handsome, isn't he, Papa?" Cathy leaned against Grace and stared after him.

"A decent-looking lad." Not about to risk saying more, Jack turned and strode back into the house.

Chapter Thirteen

Lottie stood at the rail of the *Highland Lass* and stared out over the gently rolling ocean. The star-studded sky and pleasant motion of the ship soothed her, easing away thoughts of the safety and security she was leaving behind and energizing her with hopes for the future.

"Good evening to you, lass." Captain James MacTavish came to join her. "A perfect night, is it not?"

He leaned on the rail beside her. "Makes a man realize he's chosen the right profession."

"You enjoy sailing." She smiled over at him.

"Oh, aye. What better way to see the world…or at least part of it. I must say I do miss the excitement I enjoyed during the war…chasing and being chased."

"A man of adventure."

"You could say that. And you, mistress? What of you? Are you, too, a person who relishes adventure?"

"Why do you say such a thing?"

"It's not often I have a lady travelling alone aboard, especially not one destined to Riverhaven." He looked over at her, and she saw his weathered countenance posing a question.

"Perhaps I am," she said after a pause, choosing her words carefully. "I'm seeking a new start. A friend who came out to that community some time ago wrote to tell me such was possible there."

"Ah, well, then, perhaps you are indeed headed for the right place." He turned his gaze back out over the rolling waves.

"Perhaps?"

"A goodly number of people have made a fresh start in the village, but mostly they've been lads with strong backs and hard spirits, like one lad I took out a while back. Good-looking, strapping lad, dark curly hair, with what I reckoned was a tough life behind him."

"Dark curly hair?" The captain's description raised a whisper of hope. "Do you recall his name, Captain?"

"Aye. It was Douglas...Douglas Smith."

"Douglas Smith." Lottie drew a deep breath. Surely this was her Douglas. He'd probably changed his last name to avoid being discovered by enemies.

"You know the lad?" The captain drew himself up and away from the rail. His eyes narrowed as he looked over at her.

"Perhaps I do. Do you know what became of him once he reached Riverhaven?"

"Got work straight off at the local tavern. Might still be there, for all I know, or he might have moved on. I left the village shortly afterwards. Well, I must be getting on. My helmsman seems to be in need of my instruction."

****

Lottie came down the gangplank and paused. What now? Was Douglas still in this primitive little community, or had he moved on? She'd had only one letter from him since he'd fled Scotland, and it had merely informed her that he had arrived safely in this village of Riverhaven in the British North American province of New Brunswick.

She hadn't anticipated the absolute rustic conditions into which she found herself. Her imagination had provided a colonial village but definitely not this crude little settlement with no houses that were more than cabin size and only one structure that resembled a store. To her left, set back from the dock, was a building with the sign "Tavern" on its side. A nasty roiling sensation rose in her stomach, and she willed herself to be calm and exude confidence.

"May I be of assistance, ma'am?"

She turned to see a tall, dark-haired man, wisps of gray at his temples, standing a few feet away from her.

"I don't mean to intrude, but you appear alone and a trifle at a loss." He smiled as she recognized he was ruggedly handsome and wore the rough homespun of a working man. "I'm a recent newcomer to Riverhaven myself. It can be a disconcerting experience."

"Thank you." Lottie Danvers was nothing if not an excellent reader of men's characters. She sensed no ill intention emanating from this stranger. "I'm looking for a man named Douglas MacMillan."

"Ah, yes. I believe he has a farm a short distance outside the town. I met him at Sunday service last week. Is he expecting you?"

"No. But he is a friend...a very good friend."

Douglas, a farmer? Was this the same Douglas MacMillan she'd known back in Scotland? The name was common enough. Perhaps this was someone else.

"Well, guid, verrae guid." She felt a rush of relief when he didn't question her explanation and even recognized her accent by responding in kind. "Excuse me. My manners have deserted me. Jack Wallace, at your service, ma'am." He executed a quick bow.

"Charlotte Dally." She'd become so accustomed to using the pseudonym it came out naturally.

"Papa." A girl drove a wagon pulled by a chestnut horse out onto the wharf.

"Cathy." He turned to her, his expression brightening. "Come and meet Miss Charlotte Dally, newly arrived in our community. Miss Dally, may I present my daughter, Catherine, better known as Cathy."

"Welcome, Miss Dally." Cathy, an outstandingly pretty teenager, smiled down at her. "I hope you had a pleasant voyage."

"As well as one could expect, thank you."

"Cathy, have you all of our supplies?" Jack Wallace walked over to glance into the wagon's bed.

"Every bit of them, Papa."

"Guid, verrae guid." Again the accent as he cast Lottie a grin full of intimate understanding.

A sailor came down the gangplank, a trunk balanced on one of his broad shoulders, a valise in his opposite hand. He plunked them down beside Lottie.

"It was a pleasure havin' you aboard, mistress." He beamed at her. "All the best to you."

"Thank you, Malony." She smiled and began to open the small reticle that hung about her wrist.

"No, no, mistress." He waved away her indication at a recompense. "Writin' those letters for me was a service I won't soon forget."

He turned and shambled hastily back to the ship.

"You've made a friend." Jack Wallace grasped the trunk, hefted it to one of his own broad shoulders, picked up the valise, and headed for the rear of the wagon.

"What are you doing?" she asked following him.

"I'm assuming you want to go to Douglas MacMillan's farm." He turned to her, a question in his raised eyebrows.

"Yes…yes…of course, but I don't want to impose. If you'll tell me where I may rent a carriage…"

"This isn't London…or Edinburgh." He chuckled, and she guessed her accent had caused him to mention the second city. "The only vehicles we have in this community that even vaguely resembled a carriage are stagecoaches, and they're reserved for multiple passengers on long-distance travel. Come along. The MacMillan farm is near our home."

"Yes, do come along, Miss Dally." The girl turned on the wagon seat, blue eyes sparkling. "It will do Papa good to spend time with a pretty lady. I sometimes fear he'll turn into a grumpy old hermit."

Surprised by Cathy's audacious words, Lottie looked up at the man beside her.

"My daughter tends to speak her mind." Jack Wallace cast Lottie a rueful grin. "I've been a widower for a number of years."

"I'm sorry for your loss."

"Life often holds some unexpected events." He shrugged, then picked up his tone as he held out his hand. "Let me help you aboard."

Lottie gazed about at her new surroundings as Jack Wallace took the reins from his daughter and guided the horse off the wharf and down the rough trail between a collection of log and clapboard structures that comprised the village of Riverhaven. However was she to manage in this crude little community? She had to find Douglas willing to help her.

"Got yourself a fancy piece, have ya, Reverend?" A slovenly-looking, bearded man leaned against the front of the building that held the sign "Angus Harris, General Merchant."

"Go to the devil, Michael Kelly!" Cathy hurled, from her seat between her father and Lottie, as they passed the man.

"Cathy, mind your manners," Jack reprimanded softly.

"But Papa…"

"Enough." He shook the reins over the horse's back and sent it forward at a slow trot. "Go along, Blaze."

"Reverend?" As they moved on up the street, Lottie glanced over at him, surprised. "You're a clergyman?"

"Yes."

"But I thought you were a farmer…like Douglas?"

"I'm both."

"She's a cut above anything I've seen in this country," the drunk yelled after them. "You importin' doxies now, *Reverend*?"

"Hold your counsel, Michael Kelly!" Cathy stood and yelled back at the man. "You're rude and obnoxious and—"

"Catherine, behave." Jack Wallace's order, although softly spoken, this time brooked no refusal.

"But, Papa—!"

"Sit." He shook the reins again over the animal's back, urging it into a gait that caused his daughter to sit abruptly. "If you won't do as you're told, you'll find yourself shoveling manure from the stable for the next week."

Lottie was surprised to see a slight grin twitching the corners of his mouth. And even more surprised when, a moment later, the girl's bellicose expression metamorphosed into a similar outlook as she sank back onto the wagon seat.

"I'm sorry, Papa," she said, "but that Michael Kelly—"

"Offers the perfect opportunity for you to learn to turn the other cheek. Go along," he urged the horse.

Lottie shifted on the seat. The drunkard's words had made the inappropriateness of her appearance in this rustic little community blatantly obvious. Her blue velvet travelling suit and elegant feather-trimmed hat made her look nothing like a normal working-class immigrant.

If she were going to hide her identity, she'd have to find clothing that would help her blend in among the women of Riverhaven.

"Douglas's farm is a bit off the main trail," Jack Wallace explained as he turned the horse down a rough lane into the forest to the left, "but I understand it's got fine arable land near a stream. I've been told he's doing well with his plan to provide produce for the lumbermen and shipbuilders."

Lottie, clutching the jolting board seat beneath her, digested this bit of information. It hardly squared with the Douglas she'd known, but then, wasn't she too attempting to change her stripes?

Her thoughts ended as the wagon rattled into a large clearing. The frame of a two-story house under construction stood directly before them, while a humble log cabin huddled at its side. Beyond was a large barn and a long field of cleared, cultivated land that stretched down to a boisterously flowing stream.

A woman appeared in the cabin doorway...a beautiful, raven-haired young woman.

"Mrs. MacMillan." Reverend Jack Wallace halted the mare, wound the reins around the whip stand, and jumped to the ground. "Is your husband about?"

Mrs. MacMillan. Douglas is married to this lovely woman?

"He's..." She began her reply, but at that moment, Douglas MacMillan himself stepped out of the barn. He paused to look at the new arrivals.

A grin that appeared to reach from ear to ear spread across his handsome, weathered face. Relief flooded through Lottie as she recognized her friend. With a whoop, he ran to the wagon and jumped onto the spokes of the wheel nearest Lottie. His strong hands circled her waist. With dizzying speed he swept her to the ground and into his arms.

"By all that's wonderful!" he cried.

"Yes," she replied a bit breathless from his greeting. "Charlotte Dally has decided to pay you a visit."

Eyes widening, a puzzled expression replacing the grin, he drew her out from him and looked down at her. It only took a moment for what she recognized as understanding dawning in his expression.

"Has she now?" The grin returned.

"Definitely." She tilted her head to one side and gave him her best coquettish smile.

He burst out laughing, then, containing his mirth, he turned to the woman in the doorway. "Morag, love, this is Charlotte…Charlotte Dally. I've told you of her. I had lodgings in her house back in Edinburgh. Charlotte, this is my wife, Morag."

"A pleasure to meet you, Mrs. MacMillan." Lottie bobbed an acknowledgement.

A curt nod was the response.

She knows. Douglas has told her the truth about me. Oh, God!

"Have you a place to stay?" His hands still on her upper arms, he was looking with concern into her face.

"I haven't yet secured lodgings." She lowered her gaze.

"Then you'll stay here with us." Douglas's response was instantaneous. "We have only one bedroom, but I'll sleep in the barn." He winked at Lottie. "It won't be the first time, will it…Charlotte. Morag and I will be honored to have you with us."

Glancing at Douglas's wife, Lottie knew such wasn't the case. Her blue eyes had become sapphire hard.

"Miss Dally's accommodations need not be a concern." Jack Wallace spoke quickly from the wagon seat. "She will be staying with Cathy and me at the manse."

"Of course." His daughter was quick to agree. "She's most welcome."

"I thank you, Reverend Wallace, but I can't impose."

"You won't. Now it looks like rain. We'd best be going."

She looked at Douglas. Their gazes met. An ocean away, they'd shared so much. They needed to talk, but not now. When they were alone.

When Lottie turned back to the wagon, Douglas hoisted her to the seat. Once she was safely aboard, he reached up to catch her hand.

"It's good to see you…Charlotte, so very good."

"And you, Douglas." She smiled down at him.

Reverend Wallace turned horse and wagon about and headed them up the trail toward the main road. She glanced back over her shoulder to see Douglas, feet planted shoulder width apart, hands on his hips, staring after them. He raised a hand in farewell.

Chapter Fourteen

"Cathy will take you inside." Jack Wallace halted the mare at the door of the gabled house. "I'll see to stabling Glory and unloading the wagon."

He climbed down and lifted her to the ground. His daughter jumped on her own.

"Come along, Miss Dally." Cathy darted up the steps and opened the door.

Lottie paused to look at the small, whitewashed, gabled house set back from the road. A barn stood at the rear in front of a field that stretched out for a distance before ending in a forested area. No church was in evidence.

As if catching her question, Reverend Wallace paused in unloading the wagon and smiled at her.

"The church is on a small island in the river." He pointed to a trail leading off to the right into the trees. "While I have no idea why the original builders chose to separate manse and chapel, I like the concept. Here, I can be a farmer without feeling I must dress as a minister every day."

"I understand." She smiled at him. "This is a pretty place."

"Come along, Miss Dally." Cathy stood in the open doorway. "I'll show you to your room. We have one which I hope will suit you."

"I'm sure it will." She followed the girl inside and

up a narrow flight of stairs to a level where three modest bedrooms held their doors open.

"This is Papa's," Cathy said, indicating the largest one. "And this is mine." She pointed to a smaller one across the hallway. "You will have the other, next to me." She led the way to a space that was little more than a cubicle housing a bed and washstand.

"I'm sorry it's so small." Cathy was suddenly apologetic. "It's the room that the former minister's serving girl occupied. She went off to Scotland with the family to help care for their young daughter."

"This will do quite nicely." Lottie moved inside, realizing her trunk would barely fit. Pegs along the wall were apparently what passed as a clothes press. "Thank you."

"You can get yourself settled in," Cathy said as her father brought trunk and valise up the stairs. "I'll start supper. We'll have a royal feast," she continued enthusiastically. "What with the supplies we purchased today and the fresh bread Mrs. O'Malley provided, it will be wonderful, won't it, Papa?"

Eyes bright, she looked at her father as he placed Lottie's luggage on the floor.

"Yes, of course it will be...although perhaps not exactly that to which Miss Dally is accustomed." He gave her hat and gown a sweeping glance.

"I'm sure it will be delicious." She flashed him a warm look. "I'll be down to help just as soon as I can find a more suitable gown among my possessions."

****

Jack watched his houseguest moving about the manse kitchen as she assisted his daughter to clean up the remains of their supper. The muslin dress she'd changed into was less elegant than the travelling suit in which she'd arrived. Still, it had the look of quality, a long way from the simple cotton or woolen dresses worn by local ladies. The moment she'd arrived downstairs, she'd covered it with an apron she'd found hanging behind a door in the kitchen and set to work assisting his daughter.

Although Cathy had at first refused her help, the woman had insisted. Shortly, she'd proved herself no stranger to housework.

Who was she, really, this beautiful, charming woman dressed as a lady of means yet with apparent household skills? He had to stifle the urge to question her. He'd always been a firm believer in letting people open up to him on their own, in their own time.

Furthermore, he'd been given reason to trust her, since she was a friend of local farmer Douglas MacMillan, brother to Brodie MacMillan, the man who'd quite possibly saved his life.

Still, he couldn't help wondering.

"There." Charlotte hung a dish towel on a peg by the hearth and turned to Cathy with a smile Jack found dazzling. "Finished. Mr. Wallace, another cup of tea?"

Indicating the pot keeping warm on the hearth, she looked over at him.

"If you'll join me," he said, realizing he wanted to spend more time with her.

"I'd be delighted. Cathy?" She looked at the girl as she reached for cups.

"No…no." Cathy threw a mischievous glance at her father. "I'm tired. I'm going to bed. It's been a busy day. Good night, Papa, Miss Dally." She bent to plant a kiss on her father's forehead. Carefully closing the door behind her, she left the room.

"She's a lovely young woman." Lottie poured tea into a pair of cups. "You must be so proud of her."

"I am." He accepted the drink and indicated a chair opposite at the table. She sat.

Silence.

"You must be wondering what brings a woman alone to this pioneer region." She cast her gaze down into her cup.

"I would be a rare person indeed if I didn't admit to a certain degree of curiosity, but I've always tried to avoid prying into anyone's past and accept them as I find them."

"An admirable trait." She raised her eyes to look at him. "But since you have taken me in, so to speak, I believe I owe you some explanation. Back in the Old Country, there was…is…a man who did me the honor of asking me to become his wife."

She paused while Jack waited patiently, although he felt an unreasonable sinking feeling in his gut.

"He was handsome, wealthy, and kind."

"But?" This time Jack couldn't contain himself as she stopped once more.

"He's an aristocrat, far above my station in life. As you've learned, I was Douglas's landlady back in Edinburgh. This man was expected to marry into his own class. My becoming his wife would have seriously damaged his position. And…"

"And?" Although he tried to prevent another question, he couldn't contain the query.

"And I didn't love him. I felt the only way to truly set him free to find an appropriate bride was to leave. He'd provided me with a wardrobe after my house was destroyed by fire. I took only what I felt absolutely necessary and promised to pay him back as soon as I found gainful employment. But please don't believe"— she hurried on, as she must have seen a knowing look come over his face—"that we were anything more than friends. He was simply a kindly, generous man."

"Who was in love with you."

"Yes, sadly, since I couldn't return the feeling." She drew a deep breath. "I thought it best that I leave. As the old saying goes, 'out of sight, out of mind.' "

"Aye, well, probably that was wise…if you truly dinnae love him." Unaccountably relieved of the possibility that she'd been seriously involved with another man, Jack let himself lapse into his Highland accent.

She laughed. She had a beautiful laugh, like a bubble of a mountain stream.

"What?" He drew himself up in his chair, aware of his words, feeling a warmth flood up his cheeks.

"Dunnae ya mean 'whit'?" She cast him a teasing glance. "Why, Mr. Wallace, I do believe you're a Highlander, born and bred."

"Right ya aire, lassie." Suddenly he was chuckling, enjoying a moment of mirth such as he hadn't for many a moon. "Ya've got me dead ta rights."

Their gazes met, and for a moment, a brief moment, Jack Wallace was flooded with an emotion, something at once both physical and emotional, toward this remarkable woman. Her eyes told him he was not alone in a mixture of feelings.

"I must be off to bed." Breaking the magic of the moment, she stood. "Thank you most sincerely, Reverend, for your hospitality. I'll not impose any longer than necessary."

With a swish of those fine skirts, she was gone, leaving him feeling unexplainably hollow and longing.

****

Lottie undressed and donned a silk nightgown. Its inappropriateness brought a sardonic quirk to her face. It felt cold against her skin. Flannel or wool would be much more comfortable in this country where there was no maid servant to keep a hearth fire going in bedrooms or bring a pan to warm the sheets.

With a shiver, she scurried into the bed and snuggled down beneath the quilts. In spite of the chill of the sheets, a comforting sensation engulfed.

She felt safe, at home, here with the vicar and his charming daughter.

The irony of her situation evoked a chuckle. Lottie Danvers sharing a house with a man of the cloth, becoming his housekeeper.

She remembered her meeting with Douglas. They had much to discuss. But not right away. Once she'd settled in and they found an occasion to be alone...

Her thoughts turned to the Reverend Jack Wallace. Handsome, strong, a gentleman but exuding a natural virility of which she guessed he was totally unaware. Instincts stirred.

Come to your senses, Lottie Danvers. He's who he is and...you're who you are. Nothing can change those circumstances.

With a sigh, she turned on her side. Weary from a long sea voyage and an astonishing first day in the new country, she slept.

Chapter Fifteen

Jack was urging the kitchen fire back to life from the overnight embers when she entered the room the following morning. Dressed once more in the simple muslin gown she'd worn the previous evening, she smiled at him.

"Good morning, Reverend," she said. "You're an early riser."

"I like mornings." He stood and moved to put another piece of split wood on the fire. "Always a fresh, new beginning."

"A lovely thought." She moved to the cupboard and began to gather up bread and butter. "I see you have oatmeal. Do you fancy porridge?"

"Miss Dally, you're a guest. I can't allow you to make a meal. Cathy will be down in a few minutes. She'll see to our breakfast."

"I'll enjoy being useful, Reverend." She continued in her tasks, placing dishes with the bread and butter on the table. "After weeks of shipboard inactivity, a bit of housework will be a joy."

"Very well." He went to the hand pump on the counter and began to prime it into life. "You'll need water for that porridge and"—he glanced over at her, a smile tugging at his lips—"for tea, for which I've a longing. You brew a fine cup, Miss Dally."

"Thank you, sir." She dipped him a curtsy, with a

twinkling smile he found absolutely charming.

****

"Papa, I'm going out to see to the animals." Cathy finished helping Lottie with the breakfast dishes and turned to her father.

"Feed them," he said as he sat relishing his third cup of tea, "but leave the cleaning to me. I'll be out directly."

"I'm perfectly capable of handling a manure fork and wheelbarrow." She tossed her head proudly. "You stay and enjoy your tea. Heaven knows it's been a long time since you had a decent cup."

"Cathy..." he began, but with a coy glance, she left the room by way of the kitchen's outside door.

"She's an amazing young woman." Lottie poured herself a cup of tea and sat down opposite him at the table.

"Yes, she is. Sometimes quite a handful, as you've observed, but still amazing. She could do with a woman's tutoring, however. I'm afraid our housekeeper in Fredericton provided a poor model of what a lady should be. As of yet, I haven't found anyone in this community to fill the role. What I have to offer in the way of recompense is hardly alluring."

"I'll be willing to take on the position... temporarily, that is...until you find someone more suitable."

"You?" John's tone revealed his astonishment.

"Although my wardrobe brands me as something more than a housekeeper, let me assure you, Reverend, I do know how to run a household. I can cook and clean. Furthermore, your daughter and I appear to get along well."

"But"—he struggled to come to grips with her offer—"I could pay you little, and…"

"My needs shall be simple. Bed and board and, if you deem it necessary, a small payment that will go to prove the legitimacy of my position here."

"Well, then…" He drew a deep breath, recognizing what a positive influence such a cultured woman could have on his daughter. "Well, then, I accept your offer, Miss Charlotte Dally…with sincere gratitude."

"Excellent." She finished her tea and stood. "Now, I'd best get to my duties." She headed for the door. "There are beds to be made up and a parlor hearth to be readied for the evening. I'll have a meal ready at midday."

When she'd gone, Jack sat back in his chair and wondered at what had just transpired. He'd hired a woman he'd known less than twenty-four hours to be his housekeeper, a woman who, from her manner of dress and demeanor, appeared a most unlikely candidate for the position and yet who, minute by minute, was proving herself capable of the tasks involved.

He stood and went to place his cup on the sideboard. Pausing, he looked out the window above it and saw his daughter in a shabby dress and half boots releasing her donkey into the pasture behind the barn. No longer a child, she needed a woman's hand to guide her. He hoped Charlotte Dally was that woman.

He went onto the front veranda and paused for a moment to drink in the beauty of the day. Although he missed visiting the university, he had to admit he didn't feel a loss of his pastoral charge in Fredericton. Even before news of his indiscretions had labeled him a heretic, he'd been uncomfortable preaching to a congregation many of whom he guessed looked down on a man they considered an upstart Scotsman. Here, he felt people were willing to accept him as he was.

He squinted into the early morning sun as he saw a horse and rider approaching. The prancing black mare with silver mane and tail came to stop at his doorstep while a wave of apprehension washed over him. The rider was none other than his brother, Hamish—or Harry, as he was now known.

"Good morning, Harry." He thrust his shoulders back, preparing himself for whatever his brother had to say. "Will you step down?"

"No, I will not. What I have to say will take but a minute. I've learned my son—stepson—Geordie has been visiting your lass. I do not approve. The less interaction between our families, the better."

"Have you forbidden this young man seeing my daughter?" Annoyance chaffing him, Jack faced the man on the cavorting horse. His brother had always taken charge of any situation and had never listened easily to another's point of view.

"I have, but like all my sons, he's strong willed and determined. I want your word that you will not tolerate his visiting ever again."

"Cathy will be seventeen next week, and I've always listened to her wishes. I will not send word to your lad that he's not to see my daughter unless I'm convinced it's in her best interest."

"Bah! You're as stubborn as you ever were!" Harry swung the mare about, her hooves churning up the earth. "Rest assured, if I catch my son anywhere near your lass, he'll pay dearly."

He put his heels to his mount's sides, and she bolted off down the lane to the road.

So that was how things were to be between them. A bitterness that extended to their children, a bitterness that could easily grow into a nasty canker.

Chapter Sixteen

"Minister." The man's voice made Jack turn from closing the church door. His congregation had left, and only Cathy remained waiting for him at the foot of the steps. She, too, had turned toward the speaker.

Jack saw a tall, powerful-looking Indian standing off to his right, accompanied by a woman with a child by her side.

"Welcome," he greeted them. "What can I do for you?"

"We wish to be married," the native woman said. "In your church."

"Marie was raised in the white community, taken to your church in Montreal," the man explained. "She returned to our band later but has kept some of the ways of her upbringing. We want you to marry us, Minister."

"Of course." Jack looked at the boy standing by their sides. "There are formalities, of course, a license. It will take several days."

"Today." The man spoke with conviction. "Today or not at all."

The disappointment registered on the woman's face gave Jack pause. He thought a moment, then agreed.

"We can do it at once, if that is what you wish," he said. "I'll write out the papers later. All we need immediately is another witness. My daughter is one, but…"

"I'll go to the manse and get Charlotte." Cathy, ever the romantic, was already setting off back to the house. "I know she'll come for such an important event."

As she dashed off, Jack nodded to the couple and indicated they were to follow him into the church. He wondered if Cathy would be able to convince Charlotte to come. She'd been adamant in refusing to attend services.

His doubts vanished when shortly his breathless daughter arrived pulling Charlotte by the hand. As she dragged the woman up the aisle, Jack saw apprehension in her expression. Why was she so averse to coming into a church? Just another mystery to add to those already surrounding beautiful Charlotte Dally.

"Thank you for coming, Charlotte," he said. "This man and this woman wish to be married. I'm needing two witnesses."

"Very well." She drew a deep breath and smiled a bit uncertainly at the couple.

"Then let us proceed." Jack positioned the couple before him, their son at their side, Cathy and Charlotte off to his left. "Your name, sir?" he inquired of the tall, buckskin-clad native man.

"I'm called Runner in your community," he replied.

"Very well." Jack picked up his Bible and began a brief ceremony.

When he'd finished, he wrote a few words on a paper, asked the couple to sign, and to his amazement, both complied. He'd expected them to make a mark after which he'd write their names.

"My woman—wife—was educated in one of your schools," Runner explained, and Jack was embarrassed that his surprise at their education might have been obvious. "I carry messages between the settlements for your officials. I learned to read their words."

"Ah, so no secrets." Jack grinned.

"I wish you both well." Charlotte stepped forward. She smiled at the couple and bobbed a curtsy to the woman who replied in like manner. "Now I must be getting back to my duties. I have a meal cooking." She hesitated, looked at Jack, and continued, "Will you join us...to celebrate your marriage?"

The couple exchanged a look before Marie smiled.

"Thank you. We accept," she said.

Jack smiled his approval at Lottie.

****

After the meal and the couple and their son had left, Cathy went out to care for the animals. Jack sat at the table, watching Charlotte as she finished clearing away.

"Thank you for witnessing the marriage," he said. "I was afraid you might not come. And also thank you for inviting them to eat with us. That was a kind gesture."

"I was glad to do it." Smiling, she turned to face him. "They're an amazing couple."

"They are indeed. Marie must feel her roots strongly to return to her band after growing up in our world."

"Our past always colors our future and present...or taints it." She turned back to putting dishes away in the sideboard.

"Aye, that it does." His words were slow,

thoughtful. "Charlotte, is it something in your past that prevents your coming to services? I will not ask details. I'd simply like not to think of you as an agnostic."

She faced him. "I definitely am not an agnostic." She turned and went out of the room, closing the door behind her. Jack was left with no more knowledge of her than he'd previously had.

Chapter Seventeen

"Lottie."

Recognizing his voice, Lottie turned from where she'd been weeding the vegetable garden behind the manse. An apron she'd found hanging in the kitchen covered her muslin gown. Douglas MacMillan, mounted on a fine dappled gray, grinned at her. Brushing soil from her clothing and hands, she stood to smile at him.

"Charlotte," she corrected softly.

"Oh, aye, Charlotte." He swung to the ground. "Whatever name you choose to use, it's a joy to see you. I never thought to have that pleasure again in this life."

"Nor I to be with you."

"Would you care to tell me how this reunion became possible?"

"Perhaps we might walk while I explain." She glanced meaningfully at the manse windows open to catch the spring breeze. Cathy and her father were both within.

"Over the bridge to the church?" He indicated the lane that led through a tunnel of greenery over a bridge to the chapel on the island.

She nodded and fell into step with him, the mare following at the end of her reins Douglas held in his hand.

****

"Thank the guid God that man Jeffrey Tinsdale found you." Douglas finished listening to her story as they sat on the church steps. "If I'd have been there…" He punched his right fist into his left palm.

"Douglas, you mustn't assume any blame for what happened." She put a hand on his shoulder. "There were too many of them for even you. At any rate, you had no choice but to leave, what with those blackguards hot on your trail."

"Aye, well, perhaps not." He looked back at her, and a grin slowly came over his features. "It must have been hell for that Tinsdale fellow when you refused his proposal of marriage. You're a right desirable lady, Miss Lottie."

"I didn't love him, Douglas, not as I should if I were to marry him. And after I saw Her Grace at that ball…I knew that if I'd been recognized, it would have ruined him."

"You truly didn't love him?"

"I didn't…not in the way I suspect you love the beautiful Morag."

"Aye, aye." A thoughtful smile curled his lips as he stared off across the churchyard. There was a pause before he continued. "Lottie, did you think we might marry when you set out for Riverhaven?"

"No…oh, Douglas, no." She caught one of his big, work-roughened hands in both of hers and gazed into his eyes. "I thought only to find a safe haven with a trusted friend. I love you, but as I love Jeffrey…as someone I can depend upon…as a very dear brother." She looked off toward the grazing mare. "I have yet to find what you have with Morag."

"Aye, that is right fine." He looked down at his hand in hers. "When I met her, I wouldn't even allow myself to dream that someday we might marry...she was so pure, so innocent." He stopped short, confusion in the glance he conferred on her.

"So different from the women to which you'd become accustomed?"

"Lottie..."

"It's only the truth."

"Aye, that it is." He nodded ruefully.

"Does she know?"

"Most of it, but not in any detail. She's got a romantic imagination of the world from which I came...the heroic outlaw kind of image. I've not had the courage yet to destroy those thoughts."

"A romantic who sees you as a handsome, dashing champion."

"Stop your teasin', Lottie Danvers. She's so blessed pretty, it's more likely she's a fair lady, a damsel in distress..."

"Was she in distress? Did you somehow rescue her?"

"Only from a dragon of a mama...who is now my mother-in-law." He chuckled. "Do you know, when Morag told her she was with child, the woman looked as though she'd like to take a horse whip to me."

"Were you married at the time?"

"Of course! Bloody hell, Lottie, as if I'd..."

"Quell your self-righteous indignation, laddie." She grinned over at him. "I was simply trying to understand the woman's outrage. I think you'd make a fine addition to any family."

"That's right kind of you, lass. Now enough about

me. How are you and the Reverend getting on? Not making any untoward advances, is he?"

"Of course not, you great fool!" She caught the teasing in his tone and responded in like. "He's been a perfect gentleman."

"Aye, I'd expect no less. Knowing his brother as I do, I would believe the men of that family are honorable."

"Reverend Wallace has a brother, here in this community?"

"He does. Harry Wallace. Together with Brodie MacMillan, he runs the largest milling operation in nearly two hundred miles. He's married and has seven stepchildren and a pair of twins of his own blood. Quite the New World entrepreneur and gentleman."

"Are the brothers close?"

"I understand not. A dispute back in the Highlands years ago separated them, and they've never made it up."

"How sad." She stood. "I must be getting back. I have a meal to prepare." She put a hand on Douglas's broad shoulder before he could get up. "It's lovely to have you close by. I hope my coming hasn't caused any distress to your lovely wife."

"Dunnae greet, lass." Grinning, he lapsed into deep Highland brogue as he stood. "I'll manage. I can be right charmin' when I put my mind to it."

After Douglas left her at the manse, she hastened inside. A glance at a clock in the parlor told her she had enough time to finish some housework before setting out the next meal. Picking up a rag she'd left on the post at the end of the stairs, she went into Reverend Wallace's study to tidy and dust.

As she rounded his desk, she noticed papers spread out over it. Assuming they were drafts of his next sermon, she allowed herself to glance over them.

Astonishment brought a sharp intake of breath. The words on them were definitely not those of homily. Amazed, she read on. Only the sound of the kitchen door opening made her pause. He must not discover her reading his secret papers...papers she realized could seriously jeopardize his future as a clergyman.

"I'll have your dinner ready directly," she said as she passed him in the hallway. She hoped her words didn't sound hasty or guilty.

"No need for haste." He turned to watch her as she made for the kitchen. "I have readings to do."

Readings of those shocking papers she'd discovered on his desk? As she set about preparing food, she reflected on his writings and what their implications would be if they were made public. She was not the only one with secrets, she thought.

Chapter Eighteen

Reverend Jack Wallace paused in composing his homily. Looking out his study window, he saw Charlotte Dally helping Cathy brush her donkey. Grace appeared to be basking in the attention, moving her rump to and fro the better to receive the grooming. His daughter and the woman were laughing.

With a smiling shake of his head, he returned to his task. It did his heart good to see Cathy enjoying the company of a clever, kindly, charming woman. His daughter had spent too much of her youth with the bitter, conniving Mrs. Keen. Furthermore, Charlotte Dally was proving to be an excellent housekeeper and cook. Fortune had indeed smiled on him the day he'd met her on the wharf.

He paused again to gaze at the pair. But exactly who was Charlotte Dally? He prided himself on accepting people as he found them, but this woman...she fascinated him, intrigued him, puzzled him as none he'd ever known.

He'd loved his wife, had known her to be a truly decent woman with a kind, generous heart, had thought her to be one of the finest individuals he'd ever encountered. But this beautiful, vivacious creature...

Sometimes, when she cast him one of her glances, he felt himself stirred as a man to the depth of his soul. And instantly chided himself. Lust must not be acknowledged.

He was equally certain those seductive glances weren't intentional, that they were reflexive. Yet she had the deportment of a lady...

He hoped she hadn't seen those documents he'd carelessly left on his desk. Certainly they would be enough to alter her opinion of him as a respectable clergyman. But, no, she couldn't have. He'd seen nothing moved in his study nor detected any change in her demeanor toward him.

Enough speculation. He shook his head to clear away such thoughts and went back to his sermon.

Chapter Nineteen

Lottie walked down the dusty trail to the village. The distance was proving more than she'd bargained for. On the day of her arrival, she'd been so absorbed in looking about at her surroundings, she'd taken scant note of the distance they'd travelled from Riverhaven to the manse. But today she was hot, and her feet hurt.

She'd reckoned that after the noon meal, with the Reverend and Cathy engaged in planting a field of wheat a quarter mile distant from the house, she'd have sufficient time to get to the village and back before they missed her. Now she wasn't sure.

She wondered if her decision to make a private visit to the settlement to purchase material for more suitable dresses had been a wise one. The fine muslin gown she was wearing was dusty around the bottom. In a most unladylike fashion, perspiration trickled down between her breasts.

The sound of a wagon approaching made her step to one side and pause. As it drew abreast of her, the female driver pulled its team to a stop.

"May I offer you a ride? It's a warm day for walking. I'm headed into the village, if that's your destination."

She smiled down at Lottie. She wore a shirt, breeches, riding boots, and a wide-brimmed hat.

Louisa MacMillan. This has to be Louisa

MacMillan, the woman Cathy described so vividly as one of her and her father's rescuers on their arrival in the area. Beautiful, absolutely beautiful...as beautiful as an angel, with hair the color of gold in a sunset.

"Yes, you may." Lottie hurried to climb awkwardly up onto the wagon seat beside the woman. "I'm Charlotte Dally. I'm currently staying at the vicarage."

"Louisa MacMillan." The woman clucked the team back into motion. "It's a pleasure to meet you...especially since, I understand, you're a friend of my brother-in-law."

"Your brother-in-law?" Lottie glanced over at her. MacMillan was a common name. She'd not for a moment suspected a relationship.

"Douglas. News travels surprisingly fast in this small community." She grinned. "I hope you'll like Riverhaven and decide to stay."

For a time they drove in silence. Lottie was content to enjoy the beauty of the fine day and the relief from walking in the heat.

"This country is lovely," she breathed finally. "So fresh and unspoiled."

"Then you're happy here?" Louisa glanced over at her.

"I believe I will be. Reverend Wallace and his daughter have been most kind. I'm on my way to the village to purchase material to make dresses that will be more appropriate to the country." She made a rueful gesture at the gown she was wearing.

"I'm sure Angus Harris can accommodate you at his mercantile. He has a variety of dry goods, and his wife is a fine seamstress. She can make up whatever you desire. I'll stop there, and you can look over what he has to offer."

As they entered the village, a whitewashed clapboard building of apparently recent construction opposite a blacksmith's establishment caught Lottie's eye.

"What is that structure? It looks new but empty."

"It's intended as a school. Residents built it last autumn, but as yet there have been no responses to the advertisements for a teacher that were placed in the provincial newspapers over the winter."

"A shame." Lottie tilted her head to one side.

When they reached the store Louisa had mentioned, she halted her mare.

"I'll be less than an hour picking up supplies from a ship newly docked," she told Lottie. "I'll stop by on my way home, and you can ride with me. Will that be agreeable?"

"Most agreeable. I thank you." Lottie climbed down. She noticed two women staring at her as she reached the ground.

"Good morning, Mrs. Green, Mrs. Gardiner." Louisa addressed the pair politely, but the sly wink she cast at Lottie told Lottie there was mild insincerity in her words.

"Mrs. MacMillan." One of the ladies inclined her head in the barest of acknowledgements before linking her arm into her companion's and walking off, head held high.

"Douglas's mother-in-law, Hazel Green," Louisa MacMillan informed Lottie softly. "A lovely woman," she finished, a chuckle in her tone.

****

"Good morning." Lottie walked into the village's

mercantile store and smiled at the big bulk of a man standing behind the counter, an apron covering his chest and belly. "Mr. Harris, I believe?"

"Aye, lass." A smile broke over his face as he acknowledged her. "What may I do for you this fine morning?"

"I'm looking for some material, lengths of cloth, with which I may make a few practical dresses for work about the house and garden...more suitable than this." She touched the gown she was wearing, aware that it was catching his attention. "Do you have such?"

"For sure and certain. Just go behind those shelves. You'll find a nice selection on a table there."

"Thank you." She cast him another smile before she headed off in the direction indicated. He made to follow, but was stopped by the entrance of the two women she and Louisa had encountered on the street.

"And I tell you, Lillian, she's nothing more than a doxy." A woman's voice, harsh and clear, came to Lottie as she paused out of the sight of the newcomers beside the shelves of dry goods. "Much as I hate to admit it, my son-in-law knew a number of less than respectable people back in the Old Country, and she's one of them. Why, after Morag told me about the way Douglas greeted her..."

"Ladies, what can I do for you?" Angus Harris's voice interrupted the tirade.

"Tea, sugar, and a half gallon of molasses, if you please, Mr. Harris," the same voice continued. "Put it on my husband's account. He'll be in to pay shortly."

"As you wish." Lottie heard him moving about to fill the order. "Spring is always a hard time."

"Angus Harris, I hope you're not implying we

cannot afford to pay…" Her words snapped out. "Because, if you are, I'll have you know…"

"Not at all, Mrs. Green."

Lottie gathered up the rolls of cloth she'd chosen and, head held high, marched back into sight. She received a jolt of revengeful pleasure when the two women started at her appearance.

"I'll take three yards from each of these bolts, Mr. Harris, if you please." She plunked the material down on the counter. "I'd be much obliged if your wife could make up dresses suitable for house work. I understand she's an accomplished seamstress. When will it be convenient for me to visit her so I may choose patterns and she can take my measurements?"

"I'm sure she'd be happy to accommodate you right away." He took his cue from her proud stance and ignored the other two women. "We live in the back of this place. Go through the door to the left, and tell her I've sent you."

"Thank you most kindly." She started to open her reticule, then stopped and asked, "Oh, by the way, do you have any wine…French, if possible? I should like to purchase three bottles."

The slight gasp elicited from one of the two spectators gave her a flash of pleasure. Let those old biddies make what they would of it!

"Aye, aye, just in today." He reached under the counter and produced a bottle. "Fine stuff, I've been told. Will this do?"

"Very well. Is that a freshly killed goose I see hanging behind you? I'll take that as well. I'll collect it with the wine on my way out." She took several gold coins from her reticule and dropped them on the counter. "I trust this will cover my purchases."

Regal as a queen, she turned to the women, favored them with a cold, curt nod, then headed for the indicated exit.

****

She was waiting when Louisa MacMillan drew up in front of the store.

"Ready to go?" she asked. "Errands completed?"

"Yes, thank you." Lottie handed up her sack, which clanked slightly. "If you'll just take my purchases, I'll get aboard."

"Sounds interesting." Louisa held the bag as Lottie climbed up beside her.

"Part of it is for you." Lottie opened the sack and pulled out a bottle of wine. "This is for you...for so kindly giving me transport."

"Oh, my." Holding the mare's reins in one hand, Louisa accepted the gift, a smile curling her lips. "This is nice. It's been a long time since I've had a good French wine. Brodie, like a true Scotsman, fancies whisky. I should say this isn't necessary, and it isn't, but I shall enjoy it too much to be a nay-sayer. Thank you, Miss Dally."

"You're most welcome, Mrs. MacMillan." She gave the woman a warm glance. As their gazes met, Lottie decided she'd found a friend.

Louisa placed the bottle carefully at her feet, clucked to the mare, and they moved off up the street and out of the village.

Lottie settled back to enjoy the ride. Louisa MacMillan's kindness would definitely allow her time to return to the manse before she was missed.

Chapter Twenty

Lottie finished setting the table with care before standing back to admire her handiwork. She'd found a snowy tablecloth in a drawer and a set of china in a cupboard. Near its center was a bouquet of wildflowers and the bottle of wine. She could only hope neither Cathy nor her father took offense at her audacious handiwork. She simply wanted to give them both a special meal.

On the countertop, the goose cooked to golden brown waited on a platter while a pot of potatoes kept warm on the hearth. Beside it sat a container of freshly cooked greens she and Catherine had harvested that morning. Fiddleheads, the girl had informed her, and a great delicacy in the area at this time of year when fresh vegetables weren't available.

Feeling aflutter as she hadn't in a very long time, Lottie smoothed her pale blue gown, then touched her hair to reassure herself it was in order as she heard them approaching the kitchen door, laughing together.

When they stepped inside, both fell silent. Dusty and soiled from their work, they stared first at the table and then Lottie.

Have I gone too far? Have I appalled them?

"Oh, my!" Cathy was the first to respond. She moved slowly into the room, toward the table. "Oh, my!" She turned to Lottie, her face glowing. "Charlotte, it's positively lovely."

"I'm happy you like it." Although she spoke to the girl, she let her gaze go to her father. He still stood just inside the door, staring.

"This is so special!" Cathy's enthusiasm wasn't waning. "I'm going to my room, wash up, and change into my best dress. Papa"—she turned back to her father as she headed out of the room—"you must do the same...change into your best clothes."

"Aye, aye, I will." Still appearing mesmerized by the elegance of the meal set before him, Jack Wallace moved slowly forward. "I'll be along in a minute."

After his daughter had hurried off, he turned to Charlotte.

"Fine as this is, and glad I am that it has made my daughter happy, it isn't necessary. The goose alone must have cost a pretty penny."

"It was about to become too ripe." She cast him a mischievous glance. "The price was reasonable."

"Still, you didn't have to..."

"You've been most kind to a stranger, and I'm grateful." She picked up the bottle of wine and headed for the counter. "This is my humble way of showing it." She fumbled through a drawer. "Ah! Here it is. Apparently the previous minister did occasionally indulge in a libation." She cast him a smile as she drew out the corkscrew.

"Well, everything does look tempting."

She paused in opening the bottle and caught his slight flush as he must have realized the possible double inference of his remark. "I'll just be doing as my daughter advised." Ducking his head, he strode out of the kitchen and up the stairs.

As Lottie finished her effort with the wine, she chuckled. She understood men and their often awkward compliments. Reverend Jack Wallace had come very near to giving her one. As near as he was prepared to do at the present time.

Replacing the opened bottle on the table, she thought about the Reverend. She liked Jack Wallace, really liked him. He was a caring gentleman, someone she felt she could trust. And he was handsome, broad-shouldered, narrow-hipped, and with just a hint of gray showing at the temples of his curling dark hair.

She gave herself a sharp mental shake. He was a minister, and she was…

She turned back to the food on the counter and began to slice the goose.

****

As they finished the meal, Cathy stood.

"I'm really tired this evening." She stifled a yawn. "Working outdoors must be the cause. Charlotte, leave the dishes for the morning. I'll be up bright and early to take care of them." She paused to brush her father's forehead with a kiss. "Good night, Papa."

She cast Charlotte a wink, then left, closing the kitchen door with emphasis behind her.

"My daughter is clever, but subtlety isn't one of her attributes." Jack grinned over at Charlotte. "I'm sorry."

"No need to be sorry. I find her concern for you and your happiness endearing. More wine?" She picked up the bottle as she asked the question.

"Yes…aye." He held out his glass. "It's been some time since I had such a good vintage."

"So you've a refined taste," she said as she obliged.

"I was educated in Edinburgh, then spent a year in France. More recently, when I had a charge in Fredericton, I sometimes shared a libation with a professor from the university. He had a penchant for good wine. And you?"

He hoped he'd dropped in the query subtly, naturally, so she wouldn't catch any hint of curiosity.

"Douglas worked for a wine merchant," she said, avoiding his eyes. "He often brought bottles back to my house."

"Ah, yes, he was your tenant, wasn't he?" This time he failed to keep the inquiry out of his tone.

"Yes, he was my tenant." She faced him squarely. "My tenant and a very wonderful friend, nothing more. Now"—her tone lightened—"can we leave both our pasts behind and just enjoy the wine and the fire? The wind and rain buffeting the house tonight is making this a most desirable evening to be indoors, warm and safe."

"As you wish."

A hiatus of silence followed.

"How do you like Riverhaven?" he asked. "Do you think you will enjoy living here?"

"I like it very much. I believe I will be happy."

That was an opening. Shortly they fell into comfortable conversation, sometimes even laughing over sallies on both their parts, both avoiding any reference to their pasts.

As the evening drew on, Jack added more wood to the fire, Lottie opened the second bottle of wine, and time passed so pleasantly he barely noticed the hands on the clock moving toward the middle of the night. It was only when she stifled a yawn that he realized how late it had grown.

"I'm sorry." He stood. "You must be tired. Please go to bed, and I'll bank the fire for the night."

"That's an excellent suggestion." She got up and headed for the door. She paused before pushing it open and turned back to him.

"I've had a lovely evening, Reverend," she said.

"As did I." He straightened from taking a small log from the woodbox.

Their gazes met. Jack suddenly experienced emotions he hadn't felt for a woman in a very long time.

"Good night," she said softly and left the room.

****

As she undressed for bed, Lottie felt a little smile pulling at her lips. She'd enjoyed her evening with Reverend Jack Wallace. He was clever, with a delightful sense of humor. As she pulled her nightgown over her head, the thought that his being handsome and unselfconsciously virile hadn't in any way detracted from the pleasure of their evening. Those keen blue eyes, broad shoulders, narrow hips, handsome face—was there anything physically unattractive about the man?

But, she thought, as she slid into bed, could there be anything more incongruous than the pair of them? A clergyman and a...

The remembrance of the conversation of the two women in the store that morning returned, splashing cold water over her pleasant thoughts. Recalling it, she couldn't settle to sleep.

Was she jeopardizing Reverend Jack Wallace's position in the community by continuing to remain, no matter how innocently, under his roof? As she tossed restlessly, she knew she couldn't take a chance on that happening.

She remembered the empty schoolhouse and lay still. An idea coursed through her mind. Considering it, she stared up at the ceiling. It might be a solution to the problem.

Resolved to make an attempt to carry it out, she lay still and plotted how to make it a reality.

****

Jack Wallace finished banking the fire for the night and paused to stare down into the flames. It was a long time, a very long time since he'd enjoyed an evening as much as he had with Charlotte Dally. She was bright and beautiful and entirely charming.

A sardonic smile curled his lips. Of course she was. She was a lady. Much more than her wardrobe told him so. She had all the grace such a position required.

He picked up the poker from its rack by the hearth and shoved a log deeper into the languishing flames. A lady who for some reason had felt it necessary to flee her home and most probably an entirely comfortable life in Scotland. But for what reason?

As he stared into the fire, he realized he didn't care. This was a new country, a new world, a place for new starts, new beginnings. Wasn't that the case with many of Riverhaven's residents? Wasn't it the case with him?

He turned and headed for bed, the thought that Charlotte would be there in the morning enveloping him in a warm glow.

Chapter Twenty-One

Lottie waited until Reverend Wallace and his daughter had left the manse to work about the farm before she removed the apron she'd donned to cook and serve breakfast. She hurried up to her room, checked her hair in the small mirror that hung there, and rushed downstairs.

She paused only long enough to put on an old sunbonnet she'd found hanging on a peg behind the kitchen door. The hat securely tied in place by its faded ribbons, she went out the front door.

She glanced about to see if either of the other residents of the house were in sight before scuttling down the trail to the road that led to the village. Plans for her future occupying her thoughts, she was startled by the sound of hoofbeats behind her.

"Whoa!" A man on a red horse pulled to a halt beside her. "Good mornin' to you, mistress." He looked down at her, a grin crinkling his handsome, weathered countenance.

"Good morning to you, sir." She smiled up at him.

"I'm right sorry if I startled you." His expression dissolved into one of affability. "I don't often encounter anyone walking along this stretch. Brodie MacMillan, your servant, mistress." He touched his hat brim.

"MacMillan?" She squinted up at him in the sunshine.

"Aye, husband of the beautiful Louisa and brother to the fine lad Douglas. Oh, and also proud father of a fine pair of bairns."

"I know your brother well…from back in the Old Country."

"Ah, well, then, will you trust me to offer you a ride into Riverhaven? It's a fair distance, and the day is warm." He kicked a booted foot out of the left stirrup and held down a hand. "Vixen has had a good run and is ready to settle down to be a lady."

"Vixen?"

"Aye, the mare's name. And well-earned as a filly. It's only these past few months she's decided to behave. Now, will you come along?"

"Very well." His good-natured grin was hard to resist. Lottie guessed she wasn't the first woman to appreciate the appeal of this handsome man. She accepted his hand and let him propel her up behind him with a strength that gave her to understand he was not someone to be trifled with in an adverse mood.

"And your name, mistress?" he asked as they started off, her arms about his waist.

"Please excuse me, sir. I've forgotten my manners. I'm Charlotte Dally," she replied, aware of the man's muscular build. "I'm currently staying at the manse with Reverend Wallace and his daughter."

"Charlotte Dally. Aye. My wife mentioned your ridin' into the village with her."

"She was kind enough to offer me a drive. The Reverend's daughter told me about how you and your wife rescued her and her donkey from a large cat."

"Just glad we came along at the right moment. You'll find most of us in the community are willin' to help one another out. Do you mind if I urge this fine lady into a trot?"

"Not at all."

"Where in the village might you be headed, Miss Charlotte?" he asked as they jogged along.

"I'm going to the office of the village magistrate," she said. "I understand, in lieu of a lord mayor or any other such official, that he is in charge of local affairs."

"Aye, that's true. Captain Caleb Cameron and his deputy, Dunc MacDougal, are what passes as authority hereabouts. Not goin' to report a crime, are you?" Suspicion came into his tone.

"No, nothing of that nature."

"Guid, guid, verrae guid." She caught a hint of a chuckle in his words.

"You seem relieved."

"You're new to the Riverhaven area," he continued lightheartedly. "Once you've been in residence for a while, you'll no doubt hear that people tend to believe that any mischief that occurs can be traced back to me. Mind now, I said mischief, nothin' violent or nefarious. I chust have an unfortunate tendency to get myself into any nonsense that goes on. Go 'long, Vixen. We've not got all day."

He touched his heels to the mare's side, and she broke into a gentle, rhythmic lope.

As they rounded a bend, they encountered a farm wagon headed in the same direction. On the seat were a man and a woman. Brodie's mare easily overtook it. He slowed her to speak to the couple.

"Mornin', Duncan, Mrs. Green. Shapin' up to be a hot one, what do ya say?"

"Brodie, good morning to you." Lottie guessed that

the surprised look on the man's face as well as that of his wife was as much from being unexpectedly overtaken, the sound of the wagon's wheels having muffled their approach, as by the sight of her straddled behind him on Vixen.

"Headin' into the village, aire ya?" Brodie's Highland accent suddenly became heavy with a taunt Lottie didn't fail to catch.

Good Lord, isn't it enough that this couple have caught us in what might appear an unseemly position? Why is he all at once becoming deeply Highland?

"We've a bit of shopping to do," the man on the wagon seat struggled to continue a normal conversation.

"Oh, aye, aye. Well, don't let us detain you." Brodie put his heels to his mount, and she bounded off down the trail, all but unseating Lottie and leaving the couple in a cloud of dust.

****

It was nearly noon when Jack Wallace put aside his hoe and strode back to the manse. He grinned as he watched Cathy leading her donkey down to the stream. She'd worked beside him all morning, and now she was enjoying a well-deserved respite with her pet. They were happy here, and Charlotte Dally was in no small way responsible.

He was whistling as he rounded the corner of the manse and went inside. For a moment he paused. There was no sight or sound of her. Then he saw the note on the table.

"Reverend, I've gone to the village. I hope to be back around midday. I've left food on the counter for you and Cathy. Charlotte."

Gone to the village and obviously on foot on this warm day. He crumpled the paper in his hand and turned to leave. He'd harness Glory and drive in to fetch her.

The noise of a wagon approaching stopped him. A moment later, a demanding knock sounded at the front door.

One of his congregants he recognized as Hazel Green faced him on the veranda. Her husband had remained on the wagon seat.

"Mrs. Green, what can I do for you this fine morning?"

"A moment of your time, Reverend." The woman pushed into the house. "We have information of which we believe you must be made aware." To affirm her plural pronoun, she waved a hand to indicate her husband. He looked ill at ease.

"Good morning, Reverend," he murmured awkwardly, adjusting the reins in his hands.

"Good morning to you as well, Duncan. Won't you step down and come inside?"

"No, he won't." His wife stopped him as he started to accept the offer. "What I have to say will only take a moment. Afterwards, we must be back on our way to the village."

With a shrug in the minister's direction, Duncan Green settled back on his seat.

"Come in…please." He stepped aside and indicated the open parlor door.

"I'm not sure you're aware the woman you have living under your roof is not such a lady as you may think," Hazel Green began the moment they were in the room. "We've…that is, Lillian Gardiner and I…have seen her buying wine at Angus Harris's mercantile—with gold coin."

"For a fine dinner she'd planned for my daughter and myself," he replied, forcing a smile.

Apparently she has not come to this country a pauper.

"You might be able to justify that part of her behavior, but early this morning, my husband saw her riding pillion into the village with Brodie MacMillan...Brodie MacMillan!" Hazel Green's voice rose to high notes of shock. "They passed us just now heading toward the village...and stirring up a great cloud of dust in the process."

This time the woman's words did indeed give him a start. Riding with Brodie MacMillan? Although he owed the man a great deal, Harry had warned him of the man's colorful reputation. And now to hear the beautiful, charming Charlotte was riding with him... It took him a moment to regain his equilibrium.

"I'm sure Mr. MacMillan was being kind," he finally managed to reply calmly and even with a shadow of a smile. "It is a warm day and a goodly distance to Riverhaven."

"So you're defending her!" Hazel Green's face twisted with anger. "Well, I might have guessed as much, a clergyman from a big city like Fredericton, where morals are no doubt much more lax than those here in Riverhaven. I'll be going. I've done my duty."

Turning, she flounced out of the manse.

Chapter Twenty-Two

"Come in." A male voice responded to Lottie's knock on the door of the village magistrate.

She entered to find an authoritative-looking man seated behind a scarred desk. Not exactly hard on the eyes, she thought as she became aware of another tall, well-built man sitting in a chair by the wall.

"Captain Cameron?" She stepped forward as he stood, and held out her hand. "I'm Charlotte Dally. I've come to apply for the position of schoolteacher. I understand you're in need of one."

"Yes, that's true." He took her hand. His gaze roved over the fine muslin dress she was wearing. Hardly looking like someone who would be hoping to take on an ill-paying, menial position, she guessed he was thinking. Only the worn sunbonnet gave any indication of that possibility.

"I've never done such work," she continued as she carefully withdrew her hand from his. "But I'm literate and have a basic knowledge of arithmetic. I like children and believe I can give them at least a rudimentary education."

"Well..." He came out of his astonishment and indicated a chair in front of his desk. "Please be seated, Miss Dally. I think we might be able to come to an agreement." As she sat, he moved back into his chair and waved his hand to indicate the room's other occupant. "Oh, by the way, this burly fellow is my deputy, Duncan MacDougal."

The other man, who'd also gotten to his feet after her entrance, came forward and offered a large, calloused hand.

"Pleased to meet you, Miss Charlotte." He grinned. He exuded affability. Lottie cocked her head to one side and gave him one of her most disarming smiles.

"And I to meet you, Mr. MacDougal," she said.

"Dunc, take a seat," Captain Cameron remonstrated sharply when the big man remained smiling down at her.

"Oh, aye, aye." Snapping out of the spell Lottie's coquettish glance had seemingly cast over him, Dunc MacDougal retreated to his chair, but with a crooked grin continuing to curl the corners of his mouth.

I hope I can conquer this Captain Cameron as easily.

Well aware of her power over most men, she suspected the magistrate might not be so easily enamored by her charms.

The wish vanished as she smiled at the man across the desk. After his initial surprise at seeing her, he'd flashed back to being the village authority. He looked at her, blue eyes narrowing with piercing inspection.

Married. Happily. A man of the world, who knows life as well as I do, she estimated.

"Well, now, Miss Dally, since we've had no other applicants, I'm willing to give you an opportunity to demonstrate what you can do for our children," he said. "The salary is small, but there are living quarters in the rear of the schoolhouse, with a hearth for which we'll provide fuel. It also has a bed, desk, and chair. It will need a bit of cleaning. It's been empty since we built it last summer. You'll have to attend to that on your own. Here is the sum we're prepared to offer."

He scribbled numbers on a piece of paper and shoved it across the desk to her.

Good heavens! Small wonder they haven't been able to attract a schoolteacher. Only someone like myself, with other means of support, would be even vaguely interested in the post.

"That's agreeable." She looked over at him, and she saw his eyebrows raise slightly.

Surprised I'm willing to work for such a pittance.

"Good, very good." He drew a deep breath. "When would you like to commence?"

"At the beginning of next week. I wish to begin teaching as soon as possible, since I've been told the winters can be brutal and travel difficult. Probably the children will not be able to attend during the extremely cold season."

"I'll write up a contract for you," he said. "You can sign it when you return to take up residence. I assume you'll be living in the school?"

"Yes, thank you, I will."

She stood, and he followed suit.

"Where are you staying presently, Miss Dally?" Dunc MacDougal asked. She saw interest in his eyes, but recognized it for what it was.

Merely flirting. Another married man, but one with a taste for a bit of adventure. He probably has a strong wife who makes him toe the line.

"At the manse," she replied.

"You'll be needing help moving your things into the schoolhouse," he said. "I'll be at the manse bright and early Monday morning with one of the shipyard wagons to help you."

"That's most kind of you, Mr. MacDougal." She smiled. "I've few possessions...a trunk and a valise."

"Still, not an easy carry all the way to the village." He headed for the door. "Now, as to your getting back there at the moment..."

"She has transport." Brodie MacMillan appeared in the opening. "I've come to fetch her home. She rode in with me. It's only fitting I take her back."

The two men stood facing each other in a silent challenge, causing Lottie to suppress a smug smile. Even after that brutal attack, at least some of her charm was still intact.

"Thank you, Mr. MacMillan." She adjusted her sunbonnet. "Are you ready to leave?"

"Aye, that I am, Miss Charlotte." He moved aside so that she could precede him from the office. "Good day to you, gentlemen."

He touched his hat brim and cast Dunc MacDougal a smug grin. The other muttered something under his breath.

"Was your meeting with our magistrate satisfactory?" Brodie MacMillan asked as he held down a hand to assist her once more up onto Vixen.

"Quite." She stuck her foot into the proffered stirrup, grasped his hand, and swung into place. She noticed a bag tied to the saddle, apparently filled with something that weighed it down. "I'll be moving into the schoolhouse on Monday."

"You'll be needin' help with the move," he said. "I'll hitch up one of the mill wagons and..."

"No need, I thank you, Mr. MacMillan. Mr.

MacDougal has already kindly offered to assist me."

"Has he now?" Again Lottie caught annoyance in the man's tone. "Ah, well, then"—his tone lightened—"Dunc's a good lad. Married to a woman of spirit who, I've no doubt, wouldn't be above takin' a pot to his head if she ever caught him movin' out of line. Get along there, Vixen. We've not got all day."

****

Music stopped Jack Wallace as he came to the top of the drill of potatoes nearest his house. Someone was playing a violin and very well. The sound seemed to come from his front veranda.

Rounding the house, he saw his daughter seated on the steps, and beside her was young Geordie Fowler, the source of the music. He was pulling a bow across the strings of an instrument with a proficiency that amazed Jack. Someone had taught this rough country lad to play and do it well. The tune was so beautiful, so well remembered, he paused to listen. "Flow gently, sweet Afton…"

Coming to his senses, he remembered his brother's orders that the young couple weren't to see each other. He moved into a position where the lad could see him. Instantly Geordie stopped playing and jumped to his feet.

"Good morning, sir," he said politely. "I thought Miss Cathy might enjoy a tune or two." His discomfort was obvious as he shifted from foot to foot, violin and bow hanging from his lowered hands.

"I'm sure she did, Mr. Fowler." Jack decided to proceed as diplomatically as possible. "I'm also certain your father…"

Hoofbeats thundered up the lane to the manse as

Jack recognized his brother's distinctive horse. A moment later Harry Wallace drew rein in a cloud of dust before the three.

"George Fowler, you have a job at the mill. I don't appreciate your gallivanting off any time you choose. Now get on your horse and head back to work. We need every hand at this time of year, and you well know it."

"Yes, Father." Geordie turned to put violin and bow into their case. "Good morning, Miss Cathy," he muttered as he headed for his horse.

"Good morning, Mr. Fowler," she replied as he secured the container to his saddle. "I thank you for a most agreeable concert."

To Jack's dismay, she shot her uncle a belittling look.

"You've got to understand, Reverend," Harry said, his words reeking of sarcasm, "my boys and myself work six days a week, unlike you who work only one. We don't have the leisure to do as we please. Geordie, get onto that horse and try to keep up."

He swung his horse about and took off at a full gallop. Geordie swung into his saddle, touched his forelock at Jack and Cathy, and galloped after him.

"Papa, why didn't you say something?" Cathy turned on her father. "Why didn't you defend Geordie? And why didn't you defend yourself when he made that ugly remark about you only working one day a week? Why didn't you tell him you're a farmer, that you slave every day in the fields?"

"I've known your uncle for many years." Jack turned to go into the house. "He's stubborn and set in his ways. In his present belligerent mood, no one could reason with him."

"But he was nasty to Geordie. He had no right…"

Cathy followed her father, not about to let the argument rest.

"Geordie is his son. Harry is responsible for his actions."

"His *step*son, Papa!" They'd reached the relative coolness of the kitchen. "I don't think Geordie's birth father would have been so mean."

"You don't know anything of the kind." Jack grasped the handle of the pump and worked it with more vigor than necessary in an effort to contain the disgruntled feelings his brother and now his daughter had raised. "I'd advise you to put young Fowler out of your mind."

As cold water gushed out of the spout, he put a dipper beneath it, gathered water, then took a long drink.

Giving her father a final exasperated look and heaving a sigh, Cathy strode out through the back door.

As he replaced the dipper on the counter, Jack drew a deep breath. As always, his brother had the ability to raise emotions and incite people to action. This time, Harry Wallace…and his son…had chosen to disrupt him and his family.

Chapter Twenty-Three

"You can let me off here," Lottie advised when she and Brodie MacMillan reached the lane that led up to the manse.

"What kind of a gentleman would I be if I let a lady walk the last bit?" He swung the mare into the path and trotted her up to the house. Jack Wallace, about to climb onto the seat of his wagon, turned to look at them. With Blaze harnessed to the conveyance, he was dressed in his farming clothes.

"Good mornin' to you, Reverend," Brodie greeted him good naturedly. "Busy farmin', I imagine." He kicked his foot from the left stirrup, Lottie stuck her foot into it, swung her right leg over the animal's rump, and levered herself to the ground with the help of his hand.

"As a matter of fact, I've stopped for the day. When I came up to the house and found Charlotte's note about going into the village, I decided to drive in to fetch her."

"I met Miss Charlotte walkin' to the village and offered to give her a ride to and from." Brodie's affability didn't fade in the least. "It's a right warm day for travelin' afoot."

"Yes, it is." A cold politeness came into his tone. "I thank you, Mr. MacMillan. Will you step down for a drink of water…for both yourself and your mare?"

"That's kind, Reverend, but I have to be gettin' back to the mill." He indicated the sack tied to his saddle. "Walter at the forge has made a new part for one of the saws, and I have to be puttin' it into action. I bid you both good day." He touched his hat brim and turned his horse to urge it into a lope back to the road.

"Thank you," Lottie called after him. He raised a dismissive hand and kept going.

"Well." Reverend Wallace looked at her. "You had business in the village. You had but to ask and I would have taken you."

"You and Cathy were busy about the farm." She headed for the front door. "You've already been more than kind to me."

Sensing his displeasure at her riding with Brodie MacMillan, she decided not to discuss the reason for her going into Riverhaven, at the moment.

"It's not a good idea for you to go riding about with Brodie MacMillan." His words stopped her as she reached the veranda.

"And why not?"

"Because the man has a…reputation."

"Good God, he's married, with a beautiful wife and two children he told me he absolutely adores." She swung back to face him. "Surely you don't think he would try to seduce me!"

"Charlotte, the man is known for being a law unto himself. You surely don't want to associate yourself with such a rogue."

"A rogue? I'd hardly call a man who kindly took me into the village and back again with only the best of intentions a rogue."

She flounced into the house before he could catch

the small smug smile threatening to curl her lips. The handsome, charismatic reverend was jealous, or her name wasn't Lottie Danvers.

****

"Charlotte, may I talk to you?" As she was washing her hands at the basin in her room, Cathy's voice from the doorway made her turn.

"Of course, Cathy. Would you like to come in? We'll have to sit on the bed."

"I don't mind." She took the proffered seat. Charlotte dried her hands and joined her.

"What is it, Cathy?" she asked gently. She could see the girl was perturbed.

"Oh, Charlotte, it's Papa...and Geordie...and Uncle Harry." She turned to face her. "Mostly Papa and Uncle Harry. They're being so mean and thoughtless. They don't understand, not at all, about Geordie and me."

"Fathers and uncles rarely do seem to understand young love." Charlotte smiled. "But sometimes their advice is worth consideration."

"But Geordie is a fine man. He respects me, he..."

"Let me tell you a story, my dear. Once upon a time there was a young woman who was very much in love with a young man...or at least fancied she was. Her father was dead set against their relationship, but she wouldn't listen to him. One night she ran off with the young man."

"And they lived happily ever after." Cathy ended the tale.

"Would that were the ending. No, that young man deserted her as soon as he learned her father had disowned her, that there would be no dowry forthcoming, and no comfortable place on her father's estate. Too proud to admit she'd been wrong and return to her father's house, the young woman was left to fend for herself."

"What became of her?" Enthralled by the story, Cathy looked at Charlotte, wide-eyed.

"Well, being a resourceful young lady, she found work as a housekeeper at a manor house."

"That doesn't sound so bad," Cathy said.

"Perhaps not to you, my dear, but to a young lady who'd had any number of servants to do her bidding, it was quite a comedown. Being on duty twenty-four hours a day, always at the master's beck and call, was a major change of life."

"Well, that will never happen to me." Cathy shook her head defiantly. "Geordie would never desert me."

"Perhaps not, but it's best to take your time and get to know the young man, truly get to know him."

"Oh, Charlotte, I thought you'd understand! You're as bad as Papa!" She stood and strode indignantly out of the room.

Chapter Twenty-Four

"May I have a few minutes of your time, Reverend?" Lottie stood at his study door.

"Of course." He moved aside his papers, stood, and indicated a chair in front of his desk.

"Thank you." She glided into the proffered seat.

Everything she did was graceful, ladylike. She fascinated him.

"I've met with Captain Cameron, your magistrate and government representative." She folded her hands in her lap and confronted him with sincere brown eyes.

"Aye?" Surprised, he voiced the only word that came readily to his lips.

"I presented him with a proposal."

"Aye?" Startled, he heard himself responding like a monosyllabic parrot.

"I suggested I open the school in the village."

"The school?" Astonishment engulfed him.

"Yes. I believe there's need for such a facility. While I don't pretend to be a scholar, I have sufficient learning to tutor children in basic reading, writing, and calculation."

"What prompted this decision?" He came out of his astonishment to inquire.

"It's time I moved to my own lodgings. There is a room at the back of the schoolhouse. It will make adequate living quarters."

"Surely that's not necessary." He leaned over his desk toward her. The prospect of her leaving sucked a sudden gap in his gut.

"Surely it is. I will be moving out on Monday." She turned and left the room as gracefully as she'd entered. "I thank you for your kindness and hospitality, but my decision is best for both of us."

****

"Charlotte, tell me it isn't true!" Cathy burst into Lottie's small room. "You can't be leaving us!"

"I must, my dear." Lottie turned from placing a gown in her trunk. "It's time. I've imposed on your hospitality too long."

"Imposed! Imposed?" The girl's voice had risen to a shriek. "You've been running the house, doing more work than Mrs. Keen ever did!"

"Mrs. Keen?"

"Mrs. Keen, our housekeeper in Fredericton, the woman who ruined Papa's reputation with her gossip! The woman who…"

Cathy stopped abruptly. "That isn't the reason you're leaving, I hope…gossip. I overheard that nasty old Mrs. Green talking about you yesterday. Papa thought I was still down at the brook with Grace, but I'd come back and was in the kitchen. I could hear what that miserable old gossip had to say. I was so angry I rushed out the back door and went for a long walk in the woods."

"Calm down, Cathy." She took the girl by shoulders that were shaking with indignation. "It's simply time that I started to make my own way in this community."

"But, Charlotte, we need you here." Cathy was not

about to let the subject drop.

"The children of this area need basic education." She smiled at the irate young woman. "I want to be useful. And"—she turned back to her packing—"I've been thinking. I'll need help with the school. I was hoping you'd be willing to give me a morning or two a week to assist."

"Me?" Cathy's astonishment at the suggestion was obvious in her tone. "Me, help to teach?"

"Why not?" Lottie turned back to her. "Quite possibly, if the school becomes a modest success, you can become a full-fledged teacher."

"Oh, my!" Cathy's words reflected her happy surprise. "Oh, my. Yes, Charlotte, I'd like that very much." She started to leave but turned back. "I still wish you weren't leaving. I shall miss you very much...and I know Papa will as well."

As she listened to the girl's footsteps retreat down the hall and stairs, Lottie held a gown to her breast and wondered. Would Jack Wallace really miss her?

****

"Whoa." Jack heard the word as a rattle of wagon wheels ended near his front veranda. He got up from his chair in his study and went outside. Dunc MacDougal, seated on the bench of a cargo wagon drawn by a pair of drays, grinned down at him.

"A right fine morning, Reverend," he said, affable personality intact.

"Indeed it is, Mr. MacDougal." Jack remembered meeting the man after church service. "What can I do for you?"

"Not a blessed thing, I'm glad to say. I've come to take Miss Charlotte and her possessions to the schoolhouse. I assume you know she's about to take up residence there?"

"Yes, of course." He struggled to hide his surprise at the man's words. He would have driven her and her luggage into the village. There was no need for this big, friendly lad to have come for her. And hadn't he heard that Dunc MacDougal and his friend Captain Caleb Cameron had once been privateers? Definitely not the kind of men Charlotte should befriend.

She came out onto the veranda, dressed in the travelling suit she'd worn on her arrival in Riverhaven. Her hair was neatly done up under the hat that matched.

"Good morning, Mr. MacDougal." She smiled at him. "My luggage is packed and ready to go."

Jack felt an annoying twist in his gut. Dunc MacDougal might be a married man, but that didn't make him immune to the woman's charm. And he'd seen the way Brodie MacMillan had looked at her as she dismounted from his mare. Charlotte Dally exuded charm like sunshine on a spring morning.

"Then I'll just be getting it." Dunc MacDougal wound the reins around the whip stand and jumped to the ground. He paused, looking at Jack.

"That is, with your permission, Reverend," he said. "I'll not go entering your house against your wishes."

"Certainly. Go ahead."

"There are only two pieces," Lottie called after him as he went inside. "They're in the hallway upstairs."

"Charlotte, once again, I will say this isn't necessary." Jack could not restrain himself from interjecting. "I can drive you to the school each day. There's no need to move to what I can only guess is a less commodious living condition."

"I thank you most sincerely, Jack," she said laying a hand on his arm. "But it's for the best. Rest assured I'll be available whenever you or Cathy need me."

"Here we are." Dunc MacDougal clattered down the stairs and out the door, her trunk balanced on his left shoulder, her valise in his right hand. He placed them in the back of the wagon, then hastened to the front to help her aboard.

"Good morning, Reverend." She addressed him formally in Dunc's presence. "You've been most kind. I trust we'll meet again soon." Taking the mariner's hand, she allowed him to assist her to the wagon's seat.

Duncan took up the reins and carefully turned the team about and down the lane to the road. She half turned on the seat and raised a gloved hand in farewell.

"Papa!" Cathy came rushing around the house. "What...?" She stared after the retreating wagon. "I was down at the brook washing Grace. I didn't think she was going so soon. I didn't get to say goodbye."

"You'll see her again," he said, turning to walk back into the house. "She's only moving into the village, not out of the country."

He was disappointed to hear himself speaking with a taint of bitterness in his words.

Chapter Twenty-Five

Lottie was involved in arranging the slates that would serve as an instructional board on the wall at the front of the school room when a male voice startled her. Turning, she saw a tall, broad-shouldered man silhouetted against a blaze of sunlight in the doorway, two young boys by his side.

"Good morning," he said. "I've brought my sons to enroll…"

His words trailed off as she came to fully face him.

"Lottie?" Her name was an astonished breath.

They stood staring at each other. Then the man strode forward, a broad smile on his handsome countenance. "Lottie Danvers, as I live and breathe!"

He didn't stop until he'd gathered her into his arms in a crushing embrace.

"Harry?" she choked when he released her to arm's length to grin down at her. "Highland Harry?"

"Once upon a time." His delight in meeting her still shining, he chuckled. "Harry Wallace now—father, businessman, and farmer. Guid God!" He laspsed into the Highland accent he'd suppressed on entering the school. "Lottie, I niver dreamt of seein' you agin this side of heaven. What brings you here? Or…" He paused. "Is it something along the same lines as has brought myself and others to Riverhaven, a secret?"

"A secret." She was able to smile up at him as her

initial shock at seeing him subsided. "And you must call me Charlotte...Charlotte Dally."

"Ah, understood, but a rose by any other name is just as sweet...or something to that effect. Boys?" He summoned the two children who'd stood staring just inside the door at their father's reaction to the schoolmistress. "Come here and meet your teacher...Miss Charlotte Dally. Miss Charlotte, these are my twin sons, Billie and Adam. They're six years of age and in need of a bit of formal education."

"But, Father, you called her Lottie," the one he'd indicated as Billie spoke up. "Is that her real name, or..."

"Her real name to you two young gentlemen is Miss Dally...or Miss Charlotte, whichever she prefers. You'll be forgettin' how you first heard me address the lady or"—he faced them, hands on his hips, a formidable frown on his face—"I'll be rememberin' the privy needs cleanin'. Do you understand?"

"Aye, Father." The two words were issued in unison.

"Now go out and play. I wish to speak to your teacher...to explain to her that any nonsense you pair cause will be dealt with most seriously at home. Understood?"

"Aye, Father." The pair again agreed before dashing out of the school with loud whoops.

"They're a bit high-spirited." Harry turned back to her with a wry grin. "But nothin' I'm sure you can't handle...as you handled those redcoats that so nearly caught me. If you hadn't taken pity on me and hid me in your wine cellar, I probably wouldn't be standin' here today."

"I'm a Scotswoman, Harry. I would no less."

"And a fine, loyal one. Lottie…Charlotte, it's so verrae guid to see you agin. If there's anythin' you ever need, do not hesitate to come to me. When Brodie told me about the beautiful woman by the name of Charlotte Dally he'd met on the road to the village, I had no idea I'd be knowin' her."

"Your friend is a gentleman. He gave me a ride to and from Riverhaven on the day I applied for this position."

"Ah, well, he can indeed be such, especially where women are concerned. You've nothing to fear from Brodie MacMillan, and if you ever need someone to defend you, he's your man. Now, I must be off." His speech changed and became purely English. "I'll send my sons along as soon as you're ready to start teaching." He gave her a smiling nod, turned, and left the schoolhouse.

Hands on her hips, Lottie drew a deep breath. Life certainly was a road with many twists and turns. She'd never in her wildest dreams expected to meet Highland Harry again, never mind as a father bringing his children to her school.

****

Lottie whirled at the child's scream. It was her first day of classes. Facing her pupils, she saw three of the youngest girls standing on the benches, clutching their dresses. The other female students huddled together in a corner. Across the room, the boys were gathered in a group, giggling. At their forefront were Harry's twins, Billy and Adam.

"What is it?" she asked.

One of the girls pointed and she saw a rock snake

coiled against the rear wall.

Such an old trick but one that never failed to get a reaction. Lottie marched down the length of the room to pick up the small snake. As it coiled itself around her hand, she heard a gasp from the girls.

"It's only a harmless little creature." She turned to display it to her students. "But it has no place in a schoolroom. It is far more frightened of you than you can ever be of it." She walked toward the door. "However, since I'm certain it didn't find its own way into the classroom, I want to know who helped it."

She swung to face the twins now involved in looking down at their boots. "Adam, Billie?"

"We found it on our way to school," Adam said without raising his gaze. "We thought it would be fun to bring it inside."

"Well, it wasn't. It was a cruel joke not only on the girls but also on this poor, innocent creature. I'll take it back outside before we continue with our lessons. Billie and Adam Wallace, you will remain after class."

****

After the children had filed out that afternoon, one of the girls, a seven-year-old named Sally, remained behind. She cast a demeaning glance at the twins, who sat on a bench awaiting their punishment.

"What is it, Sally?" Lottie looked at the shy child lingering at the back of the room. "Is there something I can help you with?"

"Oh, miss!" The girl rushed forward. "You were ever so brave today, picking up that snake. We're all so proud of you."

"Thank you, Sally." Lottie smiled as she recognized that her foray with the small snake had increased her esteem in the eyes of her students. "It was only a harmless creature."

"I just wanted to tell you. Good afternoon, Miss Dally."

"Good afternoon, Sally."

Feeling a warm glow inside, Lottie watched as Sally strode out of the room, head held high. The little girl cast a belittling glance at the two boys.

"Now, Adam and Billie," Lottie addressed the pair. "I've written a note to your parents informing them of your behavior." She held out a folded paper sealed with wax. "Your father has expressed the desire to hear of any misbehaviors on your part."

"We're going to have to clean the privy, for sure," Adam hissed at his twin.

The pair looked so woebegone Lottie had to suppress a grin. She guessed that such might well be their punishment, given their father's warning.

****

"Miss Charlotte?" His voice made her look up from the work she was preparing at her desk. Duncan MacDougal stood framed in the doorway. "A moment of your time?"

"Of course. What may I do for you, Mr. MacDougal?"

"It's what I can do for you, Miss Charlotte." Pulling off his cap, he advanced into the room until he paused before her desk, a tall, powerful figure, thumbs hooked into his broad belt.

"Oh, yes?"

"I've come to issue a warning. The stagecoach that runs between here and Fredericton has been robbed, held up, to the south, by a bunch of masked men. A group of redcoats have come through town on their trail, to warn residents of Riverhaven of their possible proximity to the village. Please keep your doors and windows barred at night until I can assure you of their capture."

"Thank you. I'll follow your suggestions. Will you be involved in attempting to capture the robbers?"

"Sadly, no. That's left up to the redcoats...not that I wouldn't enjoy a good chase...but provincial authorities have decreed that Cal and I stay in Riverhaven to protect the community."

"I'm sure you'll do an excellent job." Lottie smiled. "I'll feel quite safe and secure knowing you and Captain Cameron are guarding the village."

"That's right kind of you to say, Miss Lottie." Looking down at his hands holding his cap, he shuffled his feet.

She had to stifle a smug chuckle. She still had the power to flatter a man to shyness, even this big, gruff lawman.

"Well, I'd best be going." He slapped his cap onto his head and turned away. "Mind what I've said and keep your doors and windows shuttered at night."

****

"Good afternoon." Lottie looked up from the book she'd been reading at her desk in the schoolroom in the long sunrays of late day to see a small, dark-haired woman standing just inside the doorway. Pretty in a robust way, but at the moment exuding an air of absolute defiance.

"Good afternoon." Wondering what could have brought this woman in an apparent unfriendly manner, Lottie stood and smiled. No point in inviting trouble if it could be avoided. "I'm Charlotte Dally, the schoolmistress. How may I help you?"

"You aren't exactly ugly." The woman swaggered forward, hands on her hips. "I can see why he's beguiled by you."

"Beguiled? Who?" Puzzled, Lottie stared at the newcomer.

"My husband, Dunc MacDougal, as if you didn't know!" Venom fairly flew from the woman's dark eyes and bellicose countenance. "I'm his wife, Virginia MacDougal. Well, let me tell you, Miss Dally, Dunc is a flirt, nothing more, and if you try to take him from me, you will have the battle of your life on your hands! I once served on a privateering vessel with him and learned to fight as well as the next man. I may not be as ladylike or dainty as you, but I'll wager I can take you in fisticuffs any day of the week!"

"Oh, Mrs. MacDougal, let me assure you, I've absolutely no designs on your husband." She advanced toward the woman and held out an arm to indicate one of the children's benches. "Come, sit down, please. We can talk."

The woman hesitated. Apparently unprepared for Lottie's calm response, she didn't know how to proceed.

"You mean you haven't been leading my husband on?" Still defiant but, as Lottie could see, with her anger diminishing, she remained standing as Lottie took a seat.

"Definitely not. He's simply been kind to a stranger in a strange land. Surely you would expect no less of such a fine gentleman."

She tilted her head to one side and smiled up at her

companion.

"Well…no." Her outrage melting second by second under Lottie's affable demeanor, Virginia MacDougal let her hands fall to her sides.

"Of course, you wouldn't." Lottie stood. "May I offer you tea in my room?" She indicated the door behind her desk. "The mother of one of my students has kindly sent me some lovely scones. We can share them. I'd love to hear about your privateering days. Such an accomplishment for a woman! Your husband must be so very proud of you." She stood.

"Yes, well…"

****

Later, when Virginia MacDougal left the school, she waved a warm farewell to Lottie.

"Our daughter will be here on Monday to begin her learning from you, Miss Dally," she called back before turning to scurry off toward the shipyard where Lottie suspected Dunc was working.

Lottie turned back to clear away the cups and saucers that she'd used in her tea party. Gone to make up a fight they'd no doubt had over her, she guessed. Whimsically, she wondered if Dunc bore any battle scars from it.

The more residents she met, the more she was convinced Riverhaven lived up to its name.

Chapter Twenty-Six

"Good evening, Reverend." Brodie MacMillan halted his mare in front of the manse and spoke to Jack, who was sitting on the veranda in a fading twilight. "Might I step down and have a word?"

"Certainly." Jack stood and indicated a chair. "Join me."

"Thank you." Brodie dismounted and wound his reins around the veranda railing.

As the man came up the steps, a flash of something Jack hated to acknowledge as jealousy flashed through him. Although he knew he owed Brodie MacMillan a great debt for saving his daughter from the cougar, an image of Charlotte riding pillion with the handsome, swashbuckling man made his gut contract. And then there was Dunc MacDougal, a man all too much at her beck and call for Jack's liking.

Be reasonable, Jack Wallace, be cool and reasonable. You have no claim on her…yet.

Once Brodie was seated, Jack remembered his duty as host.

"May I offer you refreshment?" He stood. "I'm afraid all I have at the moment is cold water or some ancient sherry left by the previous resident. However, if you'll be patient, I'll try my hand at tea-making."

"Thank you, no. Sit yourself down, Reverend. I can tell by your dress you've spent a day in the fields and can stand a rest." As Jack did his bidding, Brodie took a chair beside him and pulled a flask from inside his vest. "A wee dram?" He held it out to him.

Jack hesitated only a moment before accepting the offer. *Mustn't be holier than thou.* He pulled the cork and took a swig before returning it to his guest.

"Good Scotch whisky, I'd say," he acknowledged the flavor. "It's been a while since I've enjoyed such."

"Then I'll be leavin' it with you." Brodie took a drink and handed the flask back to Jack. "A man needs his tipple every once in a while...even a minister."

"No, I couldn't."

"Aye, you could. Plenty more where that came from." He thrust it deeper into Jack's grip. "Now..." He settled himself comfortably in the chair. "To the reason for my visit."

"Yes, of course. What can I do for you?"

"It's about your lass and my nephew...well, adopted nephew...Geordie Fowler. He's a fine, decent young lad with a good future in our millin' business. I'm right sorry Harry has seen fit, in his stubborn Highland way, to insert himself between the pair of them. I've come to ask you, as her father, to be more reasonable and not run the young lad off when he comes courtin'."

"Courting?" The word burst from Jack.

"Aye, courtin'. Georgie is nineteen, a man, by my reckonin', and he says your lass is seventeen. I can see nothin' more natural for a couple at those ages. I was married at Geordie's age."

"To Mrs. MacMillan...Louisa?" Surprised he looked over at the man. The children and wife he'd met with Brodie hardly seemed of an age to have been the result of a youthful marriage.

"No, no." He shook his head and stared down at his hands clasped between his spread knees. "My first wife, back in the Highlands...killed by redcoats with our child she was carryin'. We were only married a year." He looked up at Jack, and he saw the pain mirrored in Brodie's weathered face. "After that, I took up with Harry...became a bit of a lad." He forced a weak grin.

"I'm sorry...so very sorry." Jack knew the bitterness of losing family to the British army. Hadn't he and Harry lost parents and a sister.

"It was a brief marriage," Brodie continued, "but a happy one. That's why I don't want to see Harry...and maybe you as well...keepin' this pair of young'uns from the joy they're findin' in each other."

"But they're both so young," Jack tried to protest.

"Aye, aye, I'll grant you that's true, but they've both got families behind them, families that are prepared to see them through any trouble."

"I'm sorry, Mr. MacMillan..."

"Brodie."

"I'm sorry, Brodie, but I can't acquiesce to your request. Harry is dead set against their relationship, and I must say I'm not in favor of my daughter keeping company with a young lad who has been raised by Harry and no doubt shares his philosophies."

"Well, then." Brodie stood with an exasperated sigh. "I can see I'm wastin' my breath at the moment. But never fear. I'm not givin' up. A marriage between these two fine young'un's is just what's needed to mend the rift between the pair o' you hard-headed Highlanders." He went down the steps, mounted his mare, and galloped off in a cloud of dust.

****

After Brodie left, Jack sat lost in thought. He hadn't even considered his daughter was deeply involved with his brother's stepson. He didn't need this complication in his life. He most definitely had to talk to her, to explain the seriousness of her actions.

He pulled the cork from the flask Brodie had left with him and took another drink. Charlotte Dally's image gushed across his mind. He missed her, missed her acutely. All this talk of marriage had awakened thoughts he hadn't previously dared to entertain. With a deep intake of breath, he made a decision.

****

Lottie watched the children leave the schoolhouse, a smile curling her lips, a small glow of success warming her insides. It hadn't been easy at the beginning, but now a month into her teaching endeavors, she recognized that she was making progress, not only in her teaching skills but, more importantly to her, in establishing a rapport with the children. Even Harry's twins, who'd proven the most rambunctious at the beginning, had settled down and were now, for the most part, attentive students.

She was writing the next day's lessons on the board when his voice stopped her.

"Charlotte."

She turned to see Reverend Jack Wallace in the doorway.

"Jack, hello. Welcome." Genuinely glad to see him, she smiled. She'd had few encounters with him since she'd left the manse, and then they'd been formal, no more than a greeting and a nod.

True, he'd stopped by the school twice to see if he

might be of assistance to her, but on those occasions he'd had Cathy with him, and their conversations had been of a generally impersonal nature.

"May I have a moment of your time?" he asked as he advanced toward her. She noticed he was wearing his good coat and trousers. His hair appeared freshly brushed, his countenance newly shaven.

"Of course." A feeling that this was about to become an auspicious occasion flooded through her.

"Your work is going well?" he asked when he stopped in front of her.

"Very well. I'm enjoying it."

"Charlotte…" He drew a deep breath and looked down at his polished boots for a moment before raising his gaze to meet hers. What she saw in his eyes startled her.

"Charlotte," he began again. "I…" He dropped on one knee before her. "I'm finding myself at a loss for words no matter how many times I've rehearsed them in my mind. Therefore, I'll simply blurt out my question. Charlotte Dally, will you do me the honor of becoming my wife?"

Silence engulfed the small log schoolroom as, frozen with surprise, she stared down at the man kneeling before her. It was as if a great shock wave had struck her. The man she suddenly realized she loved, had loved for months now, was proposing. The man she knew she could never marry.

"Jack…" She stuttered out his name as he took her hand in his.

His expression as he looked up at her choked off words. She struggled to be able to speak.

"Jack." She wet her dry lips and felt ill. "I'm

honored by your proposal…more honored than you will ever know…but I must refuse."

"Refuse?" He bolted to his feet. "Refuse? But I thought… Why? I thought you had feelings for me, that we had a relationship we both enjoyed." His words became emotional. "Charlotte, I love you. I was so bold as to flatter myself that you might have similar feelings for me."

"I do, believe me…Jack." She caught at the hand he'd released from hers and looked up at him, pain and longing burning up through her soul. "And it's because I love you that I cannot marry you. I have a past…"

"As have most of the residents in Riverhaven." His words were fervent, his fingers tightening around hers. "As do I. That's what is so wonderful about this place. It's a chance for new beginnings, to put behind us whatever happened previously. Charlotte Dally, I don't care what went before. I only care about the here and now and the fact that we love each other and should be together."

"No!" She pulled free and dashed into her living quarters, closing the door firmly behind her.

Leaning back against the panel, she heard a few moments of silence, then the sound of his booted footsteps leaving the school. A pain like from an inserted knife twisted in her heart.

She loved Jack Wallace with every ounce of body and soul, but she could never share her life with him, could never be his wife, although she longed for it more than anything she could imagine.

Chapter Twenty-Seven

"Good afternoon, Douglas."

Jack halted Blaze behind the MacMillan farmhouse. Douglas paused half way down a long row of potatoes and looked up at him.

"Jack." He pulled out a cloth, wiped his wet face, and grinned. "I didn't realize my missing church yesterday would warrant a visit from the minister."

"It's not your absence that brings me." He swung to the ground and looped the gelding's reins over a fence post.

"Oh, aye?" Douglas abandoned his work and headed up the drill to join him.

"I'd like a few words," he said when Douglas had joined him.

"Well, then you'd best come around front. There's a bench on the porch. I could do with a bit of time out of the sun. Fancy a wee dram?" he continued, when they'd reach the veranda and mounted the steps. He leaned his hoe against the railing.

"Considering the subject I'm about to broach, most definitely." He sank down on the bench, leaned back against the clapboards, and wet his lips.

"Verrae guid." Douglas went into the house. Shortly he returned, carrying a flask and a pair of tankards. He put the latter on the veranda railing and splashed a measure into each. "From your look, I'd say this is a right serious matter." He handed a drink to Jack before sitting down beside him. "When I saw you ride up, I thought maybe you wanted a look through our new home. What with everyone pitching in, we were able to finish it in good time for Morag and her mother to get right busy making a room for our wee one. "But maybe"—he continued, grinning—"you just wanted to get away from all those females who'd invaded the manse to make clothes for our coming bairn."

"No, although I grant this mission has proven a welcome reprieve." He grinned and looked down into his drink. "Douglas"—he glanced up at his companion—"how well do you know Charlotte?"

"Why do you ask?" Douglas's eyes narrowed.

"This isn't idle curiosity." Jack fingered the handle of his tankard. He drew a deep breath and met his friend's suspicious gaze. "I've asked her to be my wife."

"Ah." Douglas settled back against the wall of his house and stretched out long legs.

"You don't appear all that surprised," he said when Douglas made no further comment.

"Why should I be? There'd have to be something seriously wrong with a lad who didn't take an interest in…Charlotte."

"She refused me."

"Ah."

"Would you stop saying that word and give me some answers?" Jack's patience was running low. "I'm in love with the woman…and she's said she feels the same about me. But there's something that's keeping her back. You knew her in Scotland. If something happened there that's making her reject me, please tell me. She's not got a husband in the Old Country, has she?"

"No, no, nothing like that." Douglas avoided his companion's look and gazed up into the trees.

"Well, then, what? Dear God, Douglas, I love the woman to distraction. I'm willing to devote my life to her safety and happiness. As her friend, don't you wish such a future for her? Or do you perhaps think I'm not worthy of her, that my situation is too humble for her? Her manner of dress certainly bespeaks of a refined past."

"Bloody hell, man!" Douglas swung on him, eyes blazing. "Don't talk daft! Your material wealth doesn't figure in this!"

"Then what…why did she reject me?"

Douglas stood, moved to the edge of the veranda, and threw back his head. He closed his eyes. Finally he opened them and turned back to Jack.

"I'd be betraying Charlotte if I explained," he said.

"I love the woman, Douglas. Don't you believe that if she accepts me, I'll do all in my power to make her happy and safe?"

"I know you would, Jack. Still…"

"Very well, I'll accept that you cannot betray her trust." He stood and came to stand beside Douglas. "But will you at least speak to her on my behalf…as her trusted friend? Assure her that her past makes no difference, that I love her unconditionally and always will?"

"That I can do."

"Thank you." Jack held out a hand, and his companion took it. "I'll pray for your success."

****

"Douglas, no! I won't marry Jack Wallace, and that's the end of it."

Lottie stacked the few books she'd been able to gather for her school and placed them on a corner of the scarred, wobbly table she used as a desk. Pausing, she looked over at Douglas and drew herself up defiantly.

"Do you love him?" In the improvised schoolroom, empty except for the two adults, Douglas was blunt.

"Douglas…" Her haughty demeanor weakened as he posed the blunt question.

"Well, do you? I expect an honest answer, Lottie Danvers." Feet planted shoulder-width apart, arms crossed on his broad chest, he faced her.

"Very well." She stuck out her chin and crossed her arms. "I do."

"Then why, in the name of all that's holy, are you refusing the man? The lad's longing for you. He's a good person, a decent man…"

"And that, as you should realize, is exactly why I can't marry him."

"Lottie, he's a forgiving man. He'll not hold the past against you."

"Even a past such as mine? Douglas, be reasonable. No, I won't marry him, and that's final."

"You're one stubborn Scotswoman, lass. All I can say is that you're passing up the probability of a fine life with a good man if you continue to refuse him. Don't let that happen."

He turned and strode out of the schoolroom.

Chapter Twenty-Eight

"Ship ahoy!" The cry came in through the windows of the schoolroom opened to catch the breeze of an early autumn day.

Her students perked up as one, eyes and expressions bright. The arrival of each ship was an occasion.

Lottie hesitated a moment, teasing the children. Then, she dropped the book from which she'd been reading onto her desk and threw up her hands.

"Go!" She laughed. "Go!"

Like a herd of wild creatures, they stood and rushed out of the schoolroom. Chuckling, Lottie took her shawl from the back of her chair, threw it about her shoulders, and followed the children. Although she was not expecting anything on the ship, the excitement of its arrival in the community brightened her spirits.

****

"Good morning, Charlotte." She started as Jack was suddenly at her shoulder, falling into step with her as she made her way toward the wharf.

"Jack, good morning." She managed a smile. "An exciting day, is it not?"

"Aye."

"You've been working in the fields?" Struggling to maintain a cordial conversation, she asked.

"Aye." He looked down at his dirty shirt and

breeches. "A farmer's work is never done."

"Important work," she said and was glad they'd reached the wharf where the sounds of the crowd rapidly assembling made further conversation unnecessary.

Captain Jamie MacTavish's *Highland Lass* had nudged up to the pier. Sailors were casting lines to shoremen, who caught them and tied them fast to posts.

"A very good morning to you, lads and lassies!" The captain himself was at the rail, a grin splitting his handsome face. "I'm taking it you're more than a tad glad to see me!"

"And who else might we be expectin', Captain, seein' as you're the only one brazen enough to chance comin' up our river during the fall storm season," someone yelled back at him.

"Ya got that right, laddie." The captain continued the good-natured banter. "As soon as my lads get the gangplank lowered, we'll start unloading some of the stuff you're spoiling for."

"Were you expecting anything?" Jack turned to Lottie when they were left alone at the back of the wharf as the crowd surged toward the ship.

"No. I simply followed my students to share the excitement. You?"

"No." He shook his head. "I severed most of my ties with the Old Country long ago."

A cry went up from the crowd near the ship. A sailor had emerged onto the deck leading a horse…a golden horse with a snow-white mane and tail. The man leading her paused on the deck to allow the spectators to take in her beauty, actually turning her about as she pranced, so that all could get a good view of her.

"Never see'd the likes of that," someone said, and a murmur of agreement went across the wharf.

Beside Jack, Lottie caught her breath. It couldn't be.

A man appeared on the deck beside the horse and her handler. Jeffrey! Sir Jeffrey Tinsdale!

He looked out over the crowd on the dock. As he recognized her, a smile spread across his face, and he raised a hand in greeting. Taking the mare's lead rope from the sailor, he quieted her with a hand to her neck. She saw his lips move in what she guessed were a few reassuring words.

When the animal stopped prancing, he led her to the gangplank and carefully down its slope to the wharf. As the people made way for him, he advanced toward Lottie, his expression so bright with anticipation it struck a shaft of pain through her heart.

Why have you come so far only to be disappointed again? Oh, Jeffrey, don't you know how it hurts me to hurt you?

The thought piercing her mind, she looked up at him as he paused before her.

"Beauty missed you, Charlotte," he said softly, holding out the mare's lead rope to her.

"Oh, Jeffrey." The two words carried all the regret and chagrin in her heart.

"No need to say more." He remained optimistic as he looked at her with a gaze she recognized as being as full of love as when he'd proposed to her in England. He thrust the rope into her hand. "Now"—he turned to the staring crowd—"perhaps someone would be kind enough to direct me to the nearest hostelry."

"Right this way, sir." One of the men was quick to

comply.

Jeffrey had left none of his aristocratic charm in England. When a sailor came down the gangplank bearing a large trunk, Jeffrey cast Lottie a deep bow before he followed the man in the direction of Frank Miller's tavern.

"We'll speak later...once I've settled in," Jeffrey called back to her.

"Shall I take the mare to Frank's stable?" Jack brought her back to the moment and the fact that he was still standing beside her.

The contrast between the two men struck her with the force of a blow...Jeffrey, even after an ocean voyage, well groomed and dressed; Jack, dirty and needing a shave, his hair tied back in a straggling queue, fresh from working in the fields.

For many women, she believed, there would be little reason to tarry over a choice between the two. But not for Lottie Danvers. Her heart belonged to Jack Wallace and always would. And she could never have him.

"What? Oh, yes, Beauty must be cared for." Still struggling to recover from the recent event, Lottie handed the lead to Jack.

"You folks had best get back to helping Captain MacTavish unload his ship." Jack turned to disperse the curious crowd. "I'm sure there's mail you've been waiting for and such."

Reminded of those possibilities, they turned back to the ship, leaving Lottie and Jack alone with the palomino mare. As the horse gently nudged her, Lottie rubbed a hand over the velvet soft nose.

"She knows you well." His gaze focused on

Lottie's face, he paused, toying with the rope in his hand.

"We were friends in the Old Country," she mumbled.

"Ah, well."

"Jack…" She tried to find words to explain Jeffrey's arrival and that of the magnificent mare but failed.

"Shall I take her to Frank Miller's stable?" he asked again, this time softly, and she caught the note of disappointment in his tone.

"Yes, yes, of course…I suppose that's what Jeffrey would wish."

"Jeffrey." The word came out short and abrupt.

"Jeffrey Tinsdale…Sir Jeffrey Tinsdale."

"Ah."

As he started to lead Beauty away, Lottie came out of her state of shock sufficiently to hurry to his side.

"Jack, it's not what you think, how it appears."

"No need to explain, Charlotte." He raised his free hand. "Your past is your own."

He upped his pace, and Lottie stopped. As he led the mare away, a thought entered her mind and stuck. Perhaps, after all, it was for the best. Let Jack think she'd been involved with Jeffrey, perhaps even been his mistress. It might lessen the pain her rejection had caused him. It might even replace it with disgust.

With something that felt like a great stone in her breast, she turned back toward the schoolhouse. She'd never have the happiness she knew she could have with Jack Wallace. She didn't deserve it.

****

"Charlotte." Jeffrey Tinsdale appeared in the

doorway of the schoolhouse an hour later. "So this is how you spend your time...now."

He stepped inside, his gleaming boots making hollow sounds on the board floor.

"Yes." She turned from tidying her desk. She forced a smile. "Welcome, Jeffrey. I'm afraid the surprise of your arrival blunted my manners on the wharf earlier."

"Not to worry." He advanced to her, caught up her right hand and pressed it to his lips. Then, raising his head, he looked at her with a gaze so full of love and caring it pained her. "Charlotte, you're even more lovely than I remember. This pioneer life agrees with you."

"Jeffrey, as I told you back in England, I can't marry you, I won't tarnish your reputation..."

"Ah, yes, back in England." He released her hand and strode across the room to stare out a window. "But..." He swung back on her. "We're not in England now, my love. Here in this beautiful, wild country, I'm simply Jeffrey Tinsdale, with no need to adhere to the pretensions of an aristocrat."

"But your estate, your tenants, your seat in Parliament..."

"The first two are in the able hands of my steward. As for my seat in Parliament...my neighbor Sir Hadly Moss will be only too glad to take it on. When we marry and return, we'll simply put forward the fiction that I came out to marry an heiress to shore up the family's dwindling fortunes."

"Jeffrey, are you in financial difficulties?" Concern for this kindly man instantly taking over, she crossed the room to lay a hand on his arm.

"Certainly not!" He chuckled. "But it will make for a plausible reason for my sudden flight to America and my return with a beautiful bride."

"But those women at the ball...surely they'll remember..."

"I seriously doubt they will. And even if they had some vague recollection, they won't dare to question the validity of the beautiful Lady Tinsdale."

"Lady Tinsdale." She let her hand drop to her side as she turned slowly away.

"Charlotte, I realize my coming has been a shock, but please take time to reconsider my proposal. I'll be staying on for a time...this indeed appears to be a beautiful country...fresh and unspoiled. Let us get to know each other again and see where that reacquaintance will lead...here where my position and past mean nothing."

"Jeffrey." She couldn't find words to refute his ideas.

"I'll visit again soon." He headed for the door. "I realize you're busy with the children at this juncture, but on Sunday morning I'll come with Beauty and my horse, which I also brought aboard the *Highland Lass*. We'll go riding. I'm sure that by now you must know some suitable bridle paths."

He went back out into the bright sunlight and down the path away from the school.

Bridle paths! How little Jeffrey knew of this country...or of her feelings for the man he'd barely noticed at the dock.

Chapter Twenty-Nine

"'Afternoon, Reverend." Alex Harris placed big hands on the scarred counter of his general store and grinned a welcome at Jack. "I've got mail for you." He turned and drew a paper from one of the pigeonholes behind him. "Come on the stagecoach yesterday evenin'."

"Thank you, Alex." He accepted the letter and looked down at the seal. From the church hierarchy in York. Aware of the shopkeeper's curious eyes, he shoved it into a pocket. He'd read it later in privacy.

"I have a list here," he said pulling a paper from his vest. "My daughter is in need of a few housekeeping supplies. I'd be obliged if you can get it together for me."

"For sure and certain." Alex Harris took it and glanced over the short number of items. "Reverend"— he glanced about the shop, empty except for the two men, leaned across the counter, and spoke softly— "there's no need to go scrimpin'. Your credit is good with me. The young lass doesn't have to go short on anything."

"I appreciate your kindness, Alex, but paying for this order isn't a hardship."

"As you wish, Reverend." The shopkeeper breathed a sigh. "But my offer will stand."

With a nod of acknowledgement, Jack turned and

went out of the store. At the corner of the building, he turned down an alleyway and pulled out the letter. He drew a deep breath before running his thumb beneath the seal. The page revealed was written on church letterhead and in the careful script he recognized as that of a secretary.

He read the words, a nauseating sensation rising in his gut. Why? He'd done nothing to arouse the ire of the church hierarchy since he'd been in Riverhaven.

He'd lost Charlotte, and now this.

Crumpling the letter in his hand, he threw his head back against the hard logs of the building next to the general store and closed his eyes.

How can I tell Cathy?

****

"Good evening, Papa." Her cheerful voice greeted him as he entered the manse, the sack of supplies in his hand. She hurried to relieve him of the burden and peek inside. "I hope my list wasn't too difficult."

"Not at all. As always, you're most frugal. Cathy, put that aside and come walk with me."

"What is it, Papa?" Her face wrinkled with concern as he took her arm to guide her outside.

****

"Papa, this is a tissue of lies!" Cathy looked up from reading the crumpled letter as they sat on the church steps. "That you and Charlotte…"

"Of course it's untrue." He bowed his head to look at his hands clasped between his spread knees. "But someone in this village has made the allegation…with another witness to support the claim. Cathy"—he turned to his daughter—"you know as well as I that any evidence of impropriety on the part of a clergyman is a serious offense. The church has a right…"

"The church has no right to accuse a good, decent man of such lies!" She jumped to her feet, eyes blazing outrage. "I'm going to write to those people and tell them…tell them…"

As he saw tears blazing in her eyes, he got to his feet to take her into his arms.

"As much as I appreciate your loyalty and faith, it would do no good. I've already been in trouble in Fredericton. This is simply the final straw." He held her out from him to gaze down into her tear-streaked face. "Now we must become practical. We'll have to move out of the manse and find some other place to live."

****

"Cathy, whatever is the matter?" Lottie turned from writing the next day's lessons on the slates attached to the wall to stare at the pale-faced girl standing in the schoolroom doorway.

"It's terrible, Charlotte." She advanced into the room and sank down on one of the benches.

"Are you ill?" She hastened to join her and take her hand in hers. "Cathy…?"

"No, I'm not ill. It's Papa."

"Jack is ill?" Something inside Lottie jumped with fear.

"He's not ill…not physically." Cathy turned wide-eyed desperation on her companion. "Charlotte, the church has taken away his position. He's no longer a minister."

"Dear God! Why?"

"Because…because…" The girl lowered her gaze to their clasped hands.

"Child, don't keep me in limbo!" Her heart racing,

Lottie had to know.

"They…the people in the church in Toronto… accused him of living in sin." The words tumbled out.

"In sin? How? In what way?" At first Lottie couldn't fathom the meaning. Finally, "Oh, no! Living with me. With my living under his roof unmarried to him, having no purpose there except…"

"I'm so sorry, Charlotte!" Cathy looked up at her, tears in her eyes. "It's a wicked *lie*, a wicked lie perpetrated by a few nasty people."

Anger gushed through Lottie's body. She had a fairly good idea who that person or persons might be. She'd make short work of setting them right.

"How did you get here, Cathy?" she asked.

"I rode Glory. Father is working in the fields with Blaze. Please, Charlotte, won't you go to him, urge him to fight these charges? Glory can carry us both."

"I'll visit your father later." She was heading into her quarters to change her clothes. "First I have some people to set right."

****

Charlotte dismounted from Beauty in the Green dooryard and paused. Much as she disliked apparently accepting Jeffrey's gift, she had needed transport.

She hesitated for a moment. Struggling for a calm demeanor, she placed her head against the horse's shoulder. Losing her temper would do little to promote the reason for her visit.

"Miss Dally." Hazel Green's voice snapped as the woman stepped out onto her back doorstep. "What do you want here? If it's my son-in-law you're seeking…"

"No." Lottie squared her shoulders as she faced the woman's cold words and expression. "I've come to speak to you about a matter I believe concerns you…and Reverend Wallace."

"Reverend Wallace?" The woman appeared taken aback. Lottie glimpsed a chink of apprehension in her belligerent stance and seized it.

"Mrs. Green, a most untrue accusation has been sent to the church hierarchy in York, and now Reverend Wallace has lost his ministry. I believe you may know something about it?"

"Me?" The word was an aghast cry.

"Yes, you. You've had bad feelings about me ever since I arrived in Riverhaven…perhaps because of what you've thought to have been a relationship between me and your son-in-law. I believe you wanted to destroy me and decided the best way was to declare me Reverend Wallace's harlot."

"It's nothing more than the truth!" Hazel Green barked. "Living with him in the manse unmarried! Disgraceful!"

"With his grown daughter as chaperone? Hardly an environment for a romantic affair."

"I have a sound understanding of your past!" The woman narrowed her eyes as she advanced toward Lottie. "I know of my son-in-law's years spent in your company. My daughter has told me all, including how he lived in Edinburgh…with you!"

"Douglas was a tenant in my house, that is true, but we were never more than friends." Her innards shuddered. How much had Douglas's wife told her mother?

"Ha!" The woman thrust her anger-reddened face toward Lottie. "People in this community have seen you going about dressed like a fancy lady. And just look at that mare you're riding. A valuable animal, if ever I saw one, brought to you by a London dandy. You weren't any hardworking landlady, my girl. It doesn't take a clairvoyant to define how you managed it!"

Recognizing that she would make no progress with the woman and her designs, Lottie inserted her foot in Beauty's stirrup and swung aboard.

"I'm sorry you've seen fit to destroy the life and career of a good, decent man." She looked down at Hazel Green. "May God have mercy on your soul."

Turning the mare about, she urged her into a brisk trot. In spite of the severity of the situation, a rueful grin suddenly twitched at her lips. She'd just flung the last words repeated to a condemned man at Hazel Green. Jack would be appalled if he knew of her threat.

****

"Jack." She stood holding the mare's reins at the head of the drill of potatoes on which he was vigorously working. A breeze had muffled her arrival. He swung to face her, abrupt in his surprise.

"Charlotte." He straightened, clutching the hoe. "Good afternoon."

"It's hardly a good afternoon…not after the news Cathy has given me."

"So she told you." He began to walk slowly toward her, his shoulders slightly stooped. "She shouldn't have done it."

"Of course she should, Jack!" The words came out sharply, a rebuke. "You and I…"

"You and I what?" He drew a handkerchief from his back pocket and wiped his perspiring forehead, facing her squarely as he stopped in front of her.

"You and I have done nothing to warrant such

censure. You cannot let gossip end your career, your calling in life!" She dithered until under the intensity of his gaze she burst out, "I love you, Jack Wallace. That gives me the right to be involved in your life."

"Yet you won't marry me." He remained steadfast in his stance and look.

"This is not the time to talk of it. What will you do? Where will you and Cathy go? I assume you'll have to move out of the manse."

"Brodie MacMillan stopped by a short time ago. He had a solution for Cathy. She'll go to live with him and his wife. They have a small cabin room on their veranda where Mrs. MacMillan's sister once stayed. Cathy will be close enough to them to be safe and yet she'll have privacy. She'll also make herself useful by tending the children while Mrs. MacMillan works either at her medical practice or her writing."

"And yourself? What will you do?"

"I was apprenticed to a farrier as a lad. Walter at the forge has offered me work and a room at the back of the place."

"Jack, this is so wrong, and I'm responsible." She faced him, regret sending an ill feeling over her. "I should have known in a small community like this how my staying with you might be regarded. I tried to reason with Mrs. Green—who, I believe, is largely responsible for the misunderstanding about our relationship—but to no avail."

"Charlotte, please don't blame yourself." He gave her a weak smile. "I've been in trouble with the church hierarchy previously. It was only a matter of time before they saw fit to rid themselves of this troublesome minister."

"Still…" She turned back to Beauty. "If there's anything I can do for you or Cathy…"

"We'll be well." He came to assist her onto the mare. His hands touching her sent small waves of pleasure coursing through her. "I thank you for your efforts."

She looked down at him, into a face she loved with all her heart. Quickly she turned her mount away and galloped off down the lane to the road, utter helplessness engulfing her.

Chapter Thirty

She returned to her work in the schoolroom, but almost instantly she had another visitor. Cathy Wallace strode into the schoolroom, hands clenched at her side, her expression harsh as Lottie had never seen it.

"So he's the reason you rejected Papa!" The words stormed out in wave of anger. "Why weren't you honest with him? Why couldn't you tell him you preferred a rich man, an aristocrat? It would have hurt him less than regaling him with some tale about how your mysterious past kept you from him?"

"Cathy, that isn't..."

"Oh, no? I met Sara Gardiner at the mercantile, and she told me all about him...a wealthy dandy who arrived from England and brought you the gift of a beautiful horse."

"Cathy, believe me, Jeffrey is not the reason I haven't seen fit to accept your father's proposal."

"Isn't it?" The girl's eyes flashed fire. "Sara said he's handsome and has fine clothes...and isn't it '*Sir* Jeffrey'? Sara said that is how the sailors from the *Highland Lass* were referring to him. I suppose it will only be a matter of a few days before you'll be leaving, as soon as he can book passage for you both back to jolly old England and his estate!"

"Cathy." She hastened to stand before the irate young woman and seize her by the shoulders. "Jeffrey is a friend, someone who was kind to me back in Scotland when I desperately needed kindness. He will never"—she paused as she looked into the young woman's angry eyes—"never replace your father in my...affections."

Catherine stared at her until Lottie thought she must be seeing directly into her soul.

"Then why?" she finally breathed, her anger deflating. "Why won't you marry him? If you truly care for him, and I know he loves you with all his heart..."

"I won't expect you to understand." She released her and turned away. "All I can tell you is that I'm doing what's best for your father."

"Very well." She heard annoyance returning to Cathy's tone. "Since you've assured me your rejection of Papa is not because of Sir Jeffrey, then I can only assume you're cruel...beastly cruel!"

"Cathy..." Lottie swung back to speak, but her accuser was crossing the schoolroom in brisk, angry strides to the door.

"Miss Wallace, to you!" she shot back as she exited the school.

Jeffrey, what have you done? She sank down into the chair behind her desk. *I've lost that child's friendship and, quite possibly, that of her father.*

****

"What an absolutely glorious day." Jeffrey was enthusiastic as he helped her mount Beauty. "I must say I'm looking forward to exploring this beautiful country with you, Charlotte." He swung onto his gelding and smiled over at her. "Which way?"

"This is a well-worn trail," she said turning Beauty toward the main road out of the village toward the

Fowler-Wallace Mills as well as to the church and manse. "It's generally busy, but today being Sunday, the work wagons won't be using it." She didn't add that, due to a lack of a pastor, there would be no churchgoers, either.

"Very well." He nudged his horse into a quicker pace as she urged Beauty to a spritely trot.

They'd ridden only a short distance along the tree-lined trail when another rider rounded a bend before them. Mounted on Blaze, Jack Wallace reined to a halt.

"Good morning to you, sir." Jeffrey, always the gentleman, touched his hat brim.

"Good morning."

There was an awkward pause as the riders held their horses to a stop.

"Jeffrey, allow me to introduce you to Jack Wallace." Lottie broke the hiatus with what she believed was the only civilized thing to do. "Jack, this is Jeffrey Tinsdale."

"A pleasure, sir." Jeffrey was all affable smiles. "We're enjoying a ride in this beautiful country. Have you lived here for some time?"

"Quite some time." Jack shot Lottie a glance. "Now if you'll excuse me, I must be on my way."

"Of course. Don't let us detain you."

Jack urged his mount past the couple, put his heels to its sides, and left at a full gallop.

"Quite an accomplished horseman," Jeffrey commented, looking after him. "But I suppose one must become adept at the skill in this country."

Lottie felt a hot blush rising up her neck as she watched him go. What must Jack think, finding her out here alone with Jeffrey, riding his gift horse, dressed in a fine velvet riding costume, one she'd brought from England.

Then she caught Jeffrey gazing intently at her. Did he see her feelings for Jack mirrored in her face?

In an effort to hide her chagrin, she put her heels to Beauty and galloped ahead down the trail. Jeffrey was swift to follow her.

****

"Good day to you." Douglas MacMillan led his gray mare into the forge and paused.

"Good day to you as well." Jack turned from where he'd been feeding the fire to face the newcomer. "What can I do for you, Douglas?"

"Lady has cast a shoe." Douglas indicated his horse's left front leg. "I was hoping you'd have time to take care of it. You or Walter." He looked around.

"Walter has gone to see Louisa MacMillan about a burn on his arm, but I'm sure I can help." Jack moved to run a skilled hand down Lady's left front leg until he could pick up her hoof. "Ah, yes. She has lost a shoe...but not by accident, I'd guess." He straightened to face his customer.

"You caught me, Jack." Douglas grinned ruefully. "I'm after making an excuse to come to have a few words with you. I met Walter on the road to the MacMillan homestead and decided it would be a good time."

"So you removed your mare's shoe..."

"In truth, it was a bit loose."

"Well, let me see what I can do." Jack started to turn back to the forge, but Douglas stopped him.

"Jack, I'd like a few words with you...about Charlotte."

"Nothing needs to be said." Jack faced him squarely, making no attempt to avoid the other's keen eyes. "She's a fine woman. I will always respect her."

"Jack, for God's sake, be a man and fight for her." Douglas's words were vehement. "She loves you, you love her. Don't let a lifetime of happiness pass you by!"

"She's turned me down, Douglas. You know it. There's nothing I can do."

"So you're going to sit by and let this London dandy woo her. Bloody hell, but you're a fool."

"Quite possibly." Jack turned away. "Now, let's see what we can do for this fine lady's hoof."

"Stubborn, stubborn...a true Wallace," Douglas muttered.

****

"You're quite decided, then?" Sir Jeffrey Tinsdale stood before her in her living quarters, his countenance a mirror of regret. "You'll not marry me and return to England?"

"I'm sorry, Jeffrey, but my answer must be no." She went to the open doorway, put a hand on its frame, and gazed across at Jack, naked down to the waist except for a leather apron, bent over in shoeing a large Clydesdale. A wistful smile came to her lips.

"It's him, isn't it?" Jeffrey came to stand beside her and follow her line of interest. "The blacksmith."

"I love him, Jeffrey," she was startled to hear herself admitting. "But"—she turned hastily to him— "if it's any consolation to you, there can never be anything between us."

"Has he expressed an interest?" Jeffrey frowned as he stared over at Jack.

"He's asked me to marry him." She turned to him.

177

"And I can only assume you refused him?"

"Yes."

"Charlotte, Charlotte." He put his hands on her shoulders. "Love is a precious emotion. Don't let it slip away."

He leaned forward and planted a chaste kiss on her cheek.

"I'll be leaving," he said, the disappointment and sadness in his voice tearing at Lottie's heart. "But if you ever need me, you have but to write or come."

"Thank you, Jeffrey." Her words cracked with tears. "I wish you well. Beauty is at the tavern's stable. I'm sure she'll be glad to go home with you."

"Perhaps, but not so glad as to remain here with you." He went down the steps, paused for a moment to glance over at Jack, then back up at Lottie.

"Farewell, my darling Charlotte," he said softly. "Take my advice and, if you truly love that man and he loves you, marry him. It's not often happiness comes within a person's reach. Don't let it slip away. Captain MacTavish's ship is about to embark for England. I shall be aboard."

An ache engulfing Lottie, she watched Jeffrey walk away down the dusty street toward the ship. A truly good, kind man, and yet it was the work-soiled man with broad shoulders glistening with sweat, working at the forge, that held her heart.

As he finished with the dray's hoof, he let it drop to the ground and, as if feeling her gaze on him, looked toward her.

"Good morning." He touched his forehead and smiled. "A fine day, is it not?"

"Very fine." She smiled back, realizing that indeed

it was. The man striding out of her life toward a ship had caused her to have an epiphany. Love was indeed a precious emotion. She'd manage a way to have Jack Wallace propose to her again, and this time she definitely wouldn't say no.

Chapter Thirty-One

A thunder of hooves made her look down the trail leading into the village. Harry Wallace and Brodie MacMillan galloped at full speed, only to rein to a dust-raising halt beside the forge. Harry's expression left no doubt he was enraged as he swung to the ground and strode into the forge.

"I hope you're happy, brother!" he yelled at Jack. "Your soft ways are the cause of this trouble."

"Trouble, what trouble?" Jack stared at his brother as Brodie MacMillan entered to stand behind him.

"My son has run off with your daughter!" The words exploded at him. "A fine mess you've allowed to happen!"

"Cathy ran off with your son?" Jack stood, stupefied. "What, when, how?"

"They took two horses my son owned and ran off like thieves into the night. Now the very least you can do is saddle up that gelding my partner here so generously gave you and take to the trail after them with us. Or"—a sneer entered Harry Wallace's tone— "were you complicit in this infamy?"

Too outraged by his brother's accusation to reply, Jack dropped the tool he'd been using and headed into the stable to saddle his horse.

****

"Richibucto! Richibucto? What in God's name

makes you think they're headed there?" Harry bellowed at Brodie as the three mounted men paused outside the forge.

"Geordie isn't a well-traveled lad." Brodie shifted in the saddle. "The only place he's ever visited is Richibucto, once, with me for mill parts. I figure, with his lady in tow, he's not likely to venture into unknown territory. From there they could either catch a packet to Halifax or join other travelers to go to Saint John."

"Well, then, let's ride...before we lose them altogether."

"Jack!" Lottie came running from the schoolhouse. "I couldn't help overhearing. Is there anything I can do?"

She stood by his horse's shoulder, her face crinkled with concern.

How lovely she is. Even in his concern for his daughter, Jack couldn't help thinking of his love for her.

"Stay here and keep a watch for her return," he replied. "If she does, try to keep her with you until I get back."

"Of course." She stepped away. "I wish you luck."

"Enough blathering!" Putting his heels to his horse, Harry sent her bounding forward. Brodie gave Jack a resigned shrug before following suit. Jack, after a final glance at Lottie, kicked his gelding to a run after them.

****

"I'm reckonin' I might have been wrong," Brodie MacMillan conceded as the trio, leading weary horses, walked down the trail that was the only street in the small settlement of Richibucto. "No one here seems to have seen a young couple that answers to their description."

"You reckon?" Harry paused to swing on his companion. "Brodie MacMillan, you're one damned pain in the arse, if ever there was one. Of course, you were wrong. Now, think! Jack, where might your lass have run to? Does she have anyone who might give her and my lad sanctuary?"

"No, no." Jack heaved a weary sigh. "The only other community with which she's familiar is Fredericton, and…"

A vision of Cathy and Professor Theodore Foley flashed into his mind. Cathy knew the elderly man to be a free thinker, someone who was likely to accept her brash actions.

This thought in mind, he turned back to his horse and swung into the saddle.

"Where are you goin'?" Harry yelled after him as he turned the tired animal back down the trail.

"To Fredericton…to find my daughter."

"Bloody hell!" Wearily Brodie climbed back into the saddle. "Well, get aboard, Harry. The man has a half decent idea. Since we have no better one, we'd best follow him."

****

"My arse is right sore." Brodie MacMillan heaved himself down on the ground beside the campfire they'd lighted by the trail. "I'm gettin' too old for these long rides."

They'd been half way to Fredericton when night and their horses' exhaustion had forced them to stop.

"Aye, well, if you'd kept proper watch over that lass while she was in your care, we wouldn't be in this predicament." Harry, hunkered down by the blaze, glared over at him.

"I did my best."

"Your best wasn't good enough, was it? Now, I'm goin' to have to see to it that my lad marries my brother's lass…much as the idea galls me."

"*Step*-lad," Brodie was quick to interject. "Not blood relatives in any way."

"Thank the guid Lord for that." Harry looked over at Jack sitting on a log on the opposite side of the fire. "You're right quiet, man. For someone whose only child has run off…"

"What is there to say?" Jack looked over him, weariness in his eyes. "I should have listened to my daughter. I should have tried to understand her feelings instead of letting myself get tangled up in old animosities that had nothing at all to do with her and the young man she's chosen."

"Argh! Always the pacifist. If you'd done as I requested and run the lad off every time he tried to visit your lass, none of this would have happened."

"You two are lookin' at this like a great mistake, a tragedy even." Brodie pulled a flask from inside his vest. "Would you have preferred them to end up like those two young people in Shakespeare's yarn, *Romeo and Juliet*?"

"And what would the likes of you be knowing about Shakespeare?" Harry shot back.

"My Louisa has a right fine collection of books, and I can read." Brodie pulled the stopper from his flask and took a pull before continuing. "I'm no' an ignoramus, Harry Wallace, even if I haven't got a fancy education."

"You were afraid they might end up like that pair

in a tragical play?" A light of comprehension was beginning to dawn in Jack's mind.

"Well, I never thought they'd go so far as suicide, but I understood the longing they felt for each other." He drew a deep breath. "I married Annie when I was nineteen and herself seventeen." He closed his eyes and sighed. "It was a magical time. One should be allowed to marry when love is young and fresh."

"Brodie—" Jack looked over at the man. "Are you saying what I think you're saying?"

"Bloody hell, why hide it any longer?" He stood and faced the other two men. "I took them to Reverend Scott on the other side of the river. They were well and truly married before they headed off to Fredericton. As if I'd let the shadow of sin hang over an innocent couple like them!"

"Bastard! Traitor!" Harry bolted to his feet. His fist shot out, catching Brodie in the jaw and staggering him backward.

"Harry, don't make me fight you." Brodie ran a hand over the injury. He turned and started away but in a split second whirled back and punched Harry squarely in his jaw.

When Harry made to reply in like, Jack jumped to his feet and stepped between the pair.

"Enough! What good is this doing?"

"Step aside, Jack!" Harry drew back a fist. "I'm not about to bow to your pacifist attitude. This bloody bastard has just admitted to getting our families forever entwined."

"And is that so terrible?" Jack met his brother's angry outlook. "Brodie did what he saw as best. Would you prefer they'd run off unwed?"

Harry hesitated.

"Well, would you?"

"No, no, I suppose not." Harry dropped his fist and heaved a deep breath.

"Guid, then, verrae guid." Jack deliberately lapsed into Highland brogue. "Now let us get some rest. Tomorrow we'll get to Fredericton and hopefully find our children. I can see nothing else to do but give them our support and blessing."

Like a pair of fighting cocks at the end of a round, both men's ire seemed to fade. Brodie dropped to the ground and, putting his head on his saddle, settled for the night. The other two hesitated only briefly before following his example.

Chapter Thirty-Two

Cathy and her young husband stood meekly in the parlor of Professor Theodore Fowler's Fredericton home and faced the three road-weary men.

"Papa, please don't be angry." Cathy was the first to speak. "I love Geordie and he loves me. We didn't want to run away, but you and…Uncle Harry…were so set against us, we didn't know what else to do."

"You could have waited until you were older, until you were certain…" Jack began, but Geordie interrupted.

"We are certain, sir. Uncle Brodie was no older than us when he married for the first time, and he said…"

"Your Uncle Brodie!" This time it was Harry who broke in. "Lad, you grew up around him for a number of years, enough years to know he's a renegade of the first water. Basing your life on his…"

"Oh, and who should I base my life on?" Anger flashed in Geordie's blue eyes. "You, Highland Harry, a notorious outlaw?"

"Hi, now, young laddie." Brodie stepped forward. "Your father was a freedom fighter, a man who risked his life time and time again in an effort to save his fellow Scots. I'll not have you speakin' thus agin him."

"Yet it's all right for him to call you a renegade?" Geordie's anger was unabated as he looked at Brodie.

"Well, I blush to say it's the truth." Brodie's slow grin cracked the tension in the room. "I've never been one to follow the rules, and while I may have been instrumental in gettin' the pair of you married young as I did, I'd not encourage you to follow any further in my footsteps."

The man's good-natured attitude broke the tension in the room.

"Papa." Cathy stepped out of the protection of her husband's arm and moved toward her father.

"Cathy." He held out his arms. With a sob, she rushed into them.

"Papa, I never meant to hurt you," she said against his dusty coat. "But I love Geordie so, and he loves me, and…"

"No need to explain." Jack held his daughter, relief flooding through him. "We've not come to separate you, only to offer both of you our blessing and hopefully take you home with us."

"The lads and I will build you a snug little cabin not far from the mill." Brodie was all-out grinning. "I know the perfect spot, back a bit from the farmhouse. What say, Harry? Isn't that a grand idea?"

"I suppose it's the best thing to do, given there's no other way out of this situation." Harry's voice was gruff. He held out his hand to his son.

Geordie hesitated before stepping forward to grasp it in his own.

"Don't expect me to go embracing you," his father muttered. "I'm still mad as hell. You've made your mother half mad with worry. You'll have to deal with her on your own. I'll not be taking your part with her."

"Yes, sir." Geordie released Harry's hand and

stepped back, a suggestion of a smile curling the corners of his lips.

"Theodore, thank you." Jack turned to the professor who'd unobtrusively reentered the room.

"No need for thanks, John." He smiled. "It was a pleasure to have these two youngsters with me...even if I was risking their fathers' wrath by doing so. I couldn't see them shelterless."

"We'll be going, then." Harry stepped forward and held out a hand to Professor Foley. "I also offer my thanks."

"The best way to show gratitude is for you to accept these fine young people back into their families and offer them all the support such a relationship can give."

"Aye, aye." Harry's words were a gravelly assent. "Now, we must be getting' back to Riverhaven. Geordie, saddle your horse and the lass's. It's a long ride, and I've no desire to have the mills shut down any longer than necessary."

"You shut down the mills?" Geordie stared at his father. "You never shut down the mills on weekdays."

"Aye, well, we figured you might just be worth it. Now get those horses. It's a long ride, and we want to get home."

"John, a word before you go." Theodore stepped forward. "I don't know if this will interest you, seeing as how your family is becoming rooted in Riverhaven. Nevertheless, I would be remiss if I didn't tell you. The university, at my suggestion, has seen fit to offer you a professorship in the natural history department. You'd be a salaried employee and entitled to a small house on the campus."

For a moment Jack stood frozen in disbelief. A professorship. An opportunity to pursue his research. A wish come true.

"Papa, how wonderful!" Cathy was seizing his arm, squeezing it as she looked up into his face, eyes bright. "Of course you must accept!"

"But you and...your husband will be returning to Riverhaven, to his work." His silent enthusiasm was quelled at the thought. "I can't leave you."

"I have Geordie to look out for me now, Papa." She smiled over at her young husband. "You can visit whenever you choose. The stagecoach runs regularly between here and Riverhaven. And now, with a new position and a house, you can ask Charlotte to marry you...again."

"I know you've a lot on your mind just now, John," the professor said. "I'm only asking you to think on it."

"I will, Theodore. I most definitely will."

"Then let's saddle up horses and ride." Brodie headed for the door. "It's a good long jaunt home, and I'm right anxious to get back to Louisa and the bairns."

****

As they rode along the road back to Riverhaven, Cathy dropped back to be beside her father, who was bringing up the rear.

"Papa, that was good news, wasn't it?" she asked, looking over at him apprehensively. "About the position at the university, and the house? Surely Charlotte cannot refuse to marry you with such a prospect ahead."

"Somehow I don't think my position is the reason she hasn't accepted my proposal, Cathy. I think the reason is much more complicated."

"But you must try again." Her tone brooked no refusal. "Please, promise me you'll try again, Papa." Her tone became wistful. "I want you to be as happy as I am."

"Very well." He couldn't help being influenced by his daughter's optimism. "I'll try, but don't get your expectations too high."

"Of course not." She cast him a mischievous smirk before urging her mount ahead to join her husband. The looks they exchanged as she reached his side reassured Jack that there was genuine love between them.

Very well, Jack Wallace. You've made a promise to your child. You must carry it out, no matter how you fear another refusal.

Chapter Thirty-Three

They reached Riverhaven the following afternoon, but it was a strangely different village. It stood silent in the sunlight, not a single soul in evidence. As they passed the tavern, Frank Miller emerged, a musket in his hands, his expression grim.

"Frank, what's happened?" Brodie drew rein in front of the big man. "Where is everyone?"

"We've had a horror in the night." He came forward to stand by the shoulder of Brodie's mare. "While most of us slept, those stage bandits rode into town, tied me up, stole my liquor supply, and then went on to rob Alex Harris's store. They left him, his wife, and the children trussed up while they continued on to their worst infamy."

"Their worst infamy?" Brodie's hand went to the pistol at his belt. "Guid God, man, whit…?"

"We didn't know until this morning, after we'd been freed." Frank Miller drew a deep breath and looked over at Jack. "When they left, they took the schoolmistress with them."

It took a moment for Jack to fully comprehend the man's words. When he did, his stomach heaved, and he barely managed to control vomiting.

"Oh, Papa, how horrible!" Cathy was by his side, reaching out to put a hand over his at the front of his saddle.

"Sweet Jesus!" Brodie, ever the man of action, was ready to respond within seconds. "Whit has been done about it? I trust our magistrate and his deputy have set out after them?"

"Aye, that they did, but they've come back, lost the trail. They felt the need to protect the village in the event those buggers decide to come again."

"Bastards!" Brodie swung to the ground. Jack wasn't sure if he was referring to the kidnappers or the local law. "We'll feed and water our horses and get after them."

"What you need is a tracker."

The group turned as one to see Runner standing behind them.

"Aye, and you're just the man." His expression brightening, Brodie swung on the man. "We'll get you a horse. I know you'll be spendin' a lot of time on foot, but when we hit a good trail, it will be faster if you have a mount. Harry, you'll take charge of this expedition." He turned to the man. "I'm good on my own, but not much when it comes to managin' a group."

"Aye." Harry Wallace instantly became Highland Harry, who'd headed a group of successful freedom fighters. He swung to the ground. "See to the horses, get a mount for our tracker, gather provisions and weapons, and we'll be off. Geordie." He turned to his son. "You'll leave your wife in Frank's care. You'll be riding with us."

Jack couldn't help being impressed by his daughter's acceptance of her father-in-law's instructions. She simply nudged her horse close to her husband's and leaned out to receive a kiss.

"Find Charlotte," she murmured to him. "She

means the same to Papa as you do to me."

"Aye."

As Jack swung to the ground to begin obeying the first of his brother's orders, he had to fight to keep an overwhelming sickness from weakening both his gut and his legs.

"Thank you," he said, facing the Indian.

"You did my wife a kindness by marrying us as she wished," he said. "It's only right I repay it."

****

"This way." Runner turned his horse to the left, down a steep gully toward a brook.

"Bastards took to water to hide their tracks." Brodie swore.

"Even in water, shallow and slow-running water such as this, there are traces," Runner said as they reached the bank. "Horses turn up stones."

"Good man," Brodie muttered as the Indian dismounted into the water. "We've got the best, Jack." He turned to the other man behind him. "We'll find them, never fear. And when we do…" His words trailed off, his hand going to the sword at his side explaining the rest.

Determined to rescue Charlotte and bring her to safety, revulsion at the probable bloodshed that would ensue went against Jack's beliefs. Yet he doubted there would be an alternative.

Chapter Thirty-Four

They came upon the cabin at dusk. A half dozen horses were tethered outside.

"A fair to middlin' fight." His hand going to the sword at his belt, Brodie shifted on his mare as the four paused in the cover of a thicket. Jack recognized the man was ready, eager for a battle.

"We'll back off a bit, tether our beasts far enough away that they won't call out to the others." Harry swung to the ground and turned his mount away. "We'll come back on foot, take them by surprise."

His companions followed his instructions, Jack with emotions racing. While he hated violence and hoped the men in the cabin would surrender without a fight, he was reasonably certain such would not be the case. He was ready to face it. He had to free the woman he loved.

When Harry, a pistol in his hand, kicked the cabin door open, six astonished highwaymen jumped to their feet.

"Don't make a move." Harry advanced inside, Brodie close at his heels, Jack, Runner, and Geordie behind him, all equally armed. "Raise your hands where I can see them."

As the men obeyed, Jack saw Charlotte on a crude bunk in a back corner. Her gown was torn to shreds, her hair a tangled mass, her face darkened with bruises.

Outrage overcame common sense.

"Charlotte!" He pushed into the cabin to reach her, crossing in front of Harry.

Taking the opportunity of the man's blocked fire, one of the outlaws sprang forward. His companions followed suit.

Gunfire rang out. As Jack reached Charlotte, Harry yelled. "Jack, he's got a knife!"

Half turning, Jack saw one of the outlaws about to plunge a weapon into his back. Harry's pistol spoke. The man wavered a moment, the knife upraised before toppling to the floor.

The brothers faced each other for a split second before Jack turned back to Charlotte and Harry swung his pistol to hit an aggressor in the face.

****

Her eyes opened, one blackened to only a slit.

"Jack?" His name was a breathed whisper over swollen lips.

The fighting was over, two of the bandits lay dead, four restrained with ropes.

"Yes, it's Jack. You're safe now." He looked over at his brother standing over the four surviving invaders, a long knife in his hand. "My brother and I are here."

"Don't!" one of the villains advised as his partner stirred as if to make a move toward Harry. "The bastard's Highland Harry. He'll stick you as soon as look at you!"

"You've got that correct, laddie." Harry stared down at them, his words a guttural snarl. "In fact, after the way you've treated this lady, I'd enjoy gutting both of you like a pair of brook trout. You're indebted to my brother for my sparing you at all. He's all for you being brought before a court. I can only hope that it will see you all hanged."

Harry turned to Jack.

"The lass?"

"She's awake, but she needs help." Jack fought the nausea churning in his gut as he realized the true nature of Lottie's injuries.

"Aye, well, as soon as we're back in the village, I'll have Brodie fetch his wife." He didn't take his angry stare off the group on the floor. "But perhaps until then, you'd best wrap her in a blanket. Louisa has told me an injured person must be kept warm."

"Aye, aye."

Lottie had once again closed her eyes, making fear grip his gut in a choking knot. Carefully he gathered her into his arms. Her moan terrified him but he continued. Once he had the ragged blanket spread out on the bed, he gently laid her on it and drew it over her. Impulsively he bent to plant a kiss on her bruised forehead.

"We must get her back to the village." Runner, who'd gone outside after the fighting, had come back into the cabin. "I've made a travois. Your horse can pull it." He looked at Jack. "Brodie told me he accepts harness."

"Aye," Jack replied, "but a travois?"

"Come outside." The man indicated the door.

Reluctant to leave Charlotte but curious to see what kind of device Runner had devised, he followed him outside.

His gelding stood harnessed between two long poles that met over his back. Behind him, a kind of sled made from a blanket offered a sort of bed that could hold a person and be pulled behind him. Jack was impressed.

"You can ride my horse and lead yours," Runner said.

"No, no." Jack was adamant. "You'll not walk back. You lead my horse on yours. I plan to walk beside Charlotte."

Instead of arguing, the man nodded and headed back into the cabin.

He understands, Jack realized. *And some people still insist on calling him and his people savages.*

****

The trip back to the village seemed interminable, and not simply because Jack had insisted on walking the distance beside the travois. His physical weariness was eclipsed by his concern for the semi-conscious woman on the drag beside him.

Each time they stopped to rest or to water the horses, he squatted beside her, smoothing the hair back from her forehead and murmuring words of encouragement.

Only once during one of these stops did she open her eyes to look at him.

"Jack." His name rasped from her lips.

"Aye, Jack...Jack who will take care of you for the rest of your life." He dropped on one knee beside her.

Seemingly comforted by the words, she closed her eyes and lapsed back into unconsciousness.

****

"Sit, laddie," Harry admonished his brother as Jack paced the forge. "Brodie will come for you as soon as his wife deems it wise for you to see her."

They were back in the village, the prisoners in the

custody of Captain Cameron's jail. Now they were waiting for news of Charlotte's condition as Louisa MacMillan ministered to her in the living quarters of the schoolhouse.

"You're right. I must have patience." Jack dropped onto a bench across from his brother.

"She's got the best physician in this country tending her," Harry continued. "Louisa MacMillan is more than a doctor. She's a healer with the knowledge of the native people as well as those of science. Have faith."

He gave his brother a sage look not without a hint of mockery that Jack understood.

When Brodie stepped into the forge a half hour later, Jack jumped to his feet.

"She's doin' well," Brodie said, relieving Jack's most acute fears. "And askin' for Douglas. I sent a village lad to fetch him."

"Douglas?" Jack recognized the disappointment in his voice even as he spoke.

Why not me? Doesn't she know...?

"Dunnae greet, lad." Brodie looked at Jack and must have seen regret registered in his expression. "She and my brother have a history. It's only natural she'd want to see her oldest friend in this community."

"Aye." Jack looked at his clasped hands, calloused and scarred from working in the forge.

"She'll want to see you by and by." Brodie clapped a hand on Jack's shoulder and gave him a reassuring look. "She's been through a lot, and she's damn far from wantin' to see a beau. Besides my wife, your lass is with her. She's bein' well cared for."

"Of course, you're right." Jack tried to accept

Brodie's explanation with good grace. Still, he couldn't help wishing it had been him Charlotte had wanted to see.

****

"Lottie." Douglas MacMillan's voice broke with emotion as he came into the room and knelt by her bed. "Sweet Jesus, Lottie."

"Douglas, you mustn't...call me...that." Her words came out as broken as her lips. "You mustn't..."

"There's only Louisa here besides us, and she's not about to go questioning whatever I call you, love."

Across the room, his sister-in-law nodded as she worked tidying the place and organizing medical supplies.

"Douglas, I need your advice," Lottie murmured. "You...must be honest."

"As I always am with you, Lottie, as I always will be."

"I...I love Jack Wallace...I feel I have to share the truth with him as only you and I know it. I do not want to die without him knowing."

"You're not going to die." He clutched at her battered hand and only pulled back when she flinched. "But if it will give you peace, then by all means, do it."

"Douglas, you know the man well. Do you think he can bear to face the truth?" Her voice rose to a croak. "Do you think he'll hate me when he knows..."

"No, he will not. He's a good man, a man schooled in acceptance and forgiveness. Lottie, if you feel it will give your soul peace, tell him all. I guarantee you'll not regret it."

"Very well. Will you fetch him...and stay with us while I tell my story?"

"Of course, but not now. When you're stronger. I'll come then and stay while you tell Jack about our past."

Chapter Thirty-Five

Lottie woke the next morning to see Ginny MacDougal entering her quarters. The woman carried a valise. Behind her, her husband came in carrying an armful of bedding.

"I've come to relieve you, child," she said to Cathy who was preparing food at the table. "You go on home now and keep an eye on that young husband of yours." She cast a reproving look at her own. "He'll need a firm hand. They all do."

"That's not necessary," Cathy began to protest, but already Ginny, having dropped her valise, was herding her toward the door.

"Well, never mind necessary." The woman threw a shawl about the younger woman's shoulders. "You're new married." She gave her a sly wink. "You should be with your man. Mr. MacDougal will drive you out to the MacMillan cabin where I've heard you have a room quite to yourself. Dunc, see to the child's getting home."

"Aye, aye." The big man cast his wife a rueful grin as he took Cathy's arm to guide her to the door.

"And then you might stop by Captain Cameron's home and see how our daughter is faring under his wife's care."

"As you wish, my angel." With a teasing nod, he guided Cathy outside and closed the door after them.

"Must keep them in check." Ginny moved to the bed and smiled down at Lottie. "Now, is there anything I can get for you, my dear? I'll be heating up some broth I've brought. As soon as you've revived from it, I'll see to changing your bedding."

"You're most kind, Mrs. MacDougal." Lottie tried to smile with cracked lips.

"Not at all. I recognized you as one such as myself on the day we had tea together. You've not had an easy life, and you can't help it that you're beautiful. Not your fault that my man had an eye for you. But not a problem. He knows better than to even consider straying. Now, to heating that broth."

In spite of her discomfort and pain, Lottie couldn't help being amused by the woman's words. Ginny MacDougal definitely was a character to best have on one's side.

****

"Jack." Turning her head on the pillow, she forced a smile as he came into the room three days later. Douglas sat on a bench at the table as Ginny MacDougal bustled about, tidying the room.

"Charlotte." He came to take a chair by her bedside and took her hand. "Thank you for seeing me."

"You're trembling," she said.

"You gave me…all of us…a great scare."

"Yes, I believe I did. I'm sorry."

"Nothing to be sorry about. It was those…"

"Please don't speak of them. Ginny, will you leave us alone for a few moments?" She spoke to the woman busily tidying the counter.

"If you're sure you'll be all right without me?" She frowned her concern.

"I'm sure."

After the woman had left, closing the door behind her, Lottie tightened her grip on Jack's hand as best she could.

"I want to tell you about my past…everything."

"Not now. You're still weak."

Douglas MacMillan remained seated at the table.

"Jack." Douglas looked over at him, a look he interpreted as sheepish on his face. "She needs to do it."

"I've summoned you both here with good reason. Please, please, just listen. Jack, I want to confess all to you in the event I die."

"You're not going to die." Douglas was emphatic. "Louisa has said you're well on the road to recovery. She said…"

"Nevertheless, when I came close to death…again, I realized I didn't want any more misunderstandings. Jack, I don't want you thinking it was anything on your part that has kept me from accepting your offer of marriage. Please," she said as he was about to protest, "I must. Douglas will verify my words."

"Very well, if it will give you peace." He drew a deep breath.

"My father had an estate in Scotland," she began. "When I was very young, no older than Catherine, I became infatuated with one of my father's farm workers. He was handsome, charming…and much too old and worldly for an innocent country girl such as I was at the time."

She paused, closed her eyes, and drew a deep breath.

"Charlotte, there's no need to explain further."

"No, you must hear it all." She opened her eyes. "I

ran off with him...to Edinburgh. We were only there a short time when I confessed to him that my father didn't plan to offer him a dowry to marry me. The following morning I awoke in the miserable room he'd rented to find him gone."

She paused as Jack saw the pain of recollection mirrored in her bruised countenance.

"Charlotte, it isn't necessary to go on," he said softly. "I don't care."

"But you must know."

"Very well."

"I didn't know what to do. I went downstairs to find my companion had left our bills unpaid. While I was listening to the landlord extolling on the evils of such young men who defiled innocent young women, an elderly gentleman came to my side. He threw gold coins on the counter. 'Will this settle the young lady's account?' he said. The man could only stare at the wealth thrust before him.

"The gentleman led me to a table and ordered breakfast for both of us. While we ate, I found him staring at me, watching my every move.

" 'You are a lady, my dear,' he said finally. 'A lady who has been foully used. Do you have plans for the future?'

"He was such a kindly old man I found myself telling him of my past and my present plight. Somehow, I managed to repress the tears that were threatening to expose the depth of my despair.

" 'Your young man was a rogue indeed,' he said when I'd finished. He paused, seeming to consider.

" 'I have a solution that I think might be beneficial to both of us,' he said finally. 'My dear wife passed two years ago. Since then, I have been hard pressed to manage my house alone. Oh, I have a reasonably competent housekeeper, but no one to act as hostess when I entertain. And I do enjoy entertaining. Even on our brief acquaintance, I recognize that you have the grace and manners of a lady. Would you consider taking on the position of hostess at Quigley Manor? There'd be no demands made on you aside from playing the part and keeping the house and larder ready for guests, I promise you.' "

"And so you agreed?" Jack's words were soft, gentle.

"Yes. And it was as he said. He had a massive manor which I ran and where I was hostess at the frequent gatherings he enjoyed. As time passed, I realized that a goodly number of his guests regarded me as his mistress, but I told myself there was no real harm in their assumption.

"Then, quite suddenly, Sir Lewis passed away, and I discovered a cousin was to inherit his lands and fortune…that is, all but a very generous allowance left to me.

"When the cousin arrived to take possession, one of his first tasks was to evict me. I had no choice but to gather up my considerable wardrobe and leave. However, in the two weeks prior to his arrival I'd had time to think about my future."

She paused to glanced over at Douglas. He nodded his support for her to continue.

"Driving through the streets of Edinburgh with Sir Lewis, I'd seen many women cast out to make a living on their own. These women hadn't been as fortunate as I. There'd been no rich milord to take them under his wing. They had no permanent roofs over their heads and definitely no one to protect them. I realized most could see but this one way of making a living which was dangerous and miserable." She tightened her grip on Jack's hand before continuing.

"Suddenly I saw a way not only to provide for myself but also to give them the shelter and safety they needed. I bought a house, outfitted it in the ostentatious manner expected of such an establishment, and took in women and girls I saw worthy of my concern."

She looked at Jack, her eyes gauging his reaction. When he merely sat quietly, she continued.

"I met Douglas quite by chance when he arrived seeking a boarding house. Once inside, he realized my home was not what he'd been seeking." She managed a weak smile in his direction, and he chuckled softly.

"We began to talk," she continued. "I decided he was exactly what I needed in the way of protection. We struck a bargain. He'd live without charge on my third floor in return for his management of security.

"The arrangement proved excellent, and we were successful. My establishment became known as the finest 'gentlemen's club' in Edinburgh. Prices excluded anyone but the wealthy, and Douglas's presence discouraged those who had ill intentions toward any of my ladies. We were very successful."

"Aye, that we were," Douglas muttered.

"Then Douglas had to leave," Lottie went on with her story. "He was in trouble with a vicious gang and had no choice but to flee to America. After he left, I hired another guard. It proved a disaster. He frequently overindulged and was useless when needed. I was trying to find a replacement for him when they came."

"They?" Jack caressed her hand gently.

"A group of thugs hired by her grace, the duchess." She tried to keep the tremble from her voice and body as she set out to tell of the horror she'd experienced. "She'd learned that not only was her husband frequently at my establishment—apparently that didn't offend her overly—but when she discovered that he'd brought their eighteen-year-old son with him, she became incensed. She wanted no slur against her boy, whom she saw as destined to a wealthy and prestigious marriage with royalty."

She paused, gathering strength to continue.

"They came to the house at midnight and attacked with all the viciousness of marauding barbarians," she said finally. "My ladies were beaten and thrown from the house, which was then set afire. Myself, they dragged into a waiting carriage and took me off to be severely beaten and left for dead in the street. That is where Sir Jeffrey Tinsdale found me...and saved my life."

"Good God!" She saw his face contort with a pained expression. "Charlotte, I'm so very, very sorry. You should have told me."

"And it wouldn't have made any difference between us? Jack, I know you're a good man, a forgiving man, but still..."

"But still he loves you, foolish woman." Douglas's expression was stern as he looked over at her. "Nothing matters to a man when he feels that way about a woman. Believe me, I know." A sardonic grin started at the corners of his mouth. "Not even the prospect of a harridan of a mother-in-law can deter a man when he's truly in love."

"That's right, Charlotte." Jack gazed over at her. The story of her past had done nothing to weaken his love for her. "I want you for my wife, Charlotte Dally. Nothing else matters...not your past, what you've recently suffered...nothing. But"—he drew a deep breath—"before you consent, you must hear my story. Then, possibly, you'll have second thoughts about me."

"Jack, I can't imagine you doing anything reprehensible." The gentleness in her eyes caught at his soul.

"Nevertheless..." He drew a deep breath and looked over at Douglas.

"If you'd rather I left..." Douglas made a move as if to stand.

"No, no. Like Charlotte, I'd prefer a witness to my story." He drew a deep breath before he continued.

"In Fredericton, my former post, I spent a good deal of time at the university, researching, and at times teaching." He paused and drew a deep breath before continuing. "My research, in conjunction with Professor Theodore Foley, involved studying the science of natural selection."

He looked into her eyes, seeking her reaction.

"I know." The two words came out softly.

"You know?"

"When I was cleaning your study one morning, I discovered one of your papers putting forward that theory."

"Were you shocked? Hardly an idea that should be entertained by a clergyman."

"Astonished." She smiled at him. "It's an amazing hypothesis, definitely one that bears further investigation."

"You really think so?" Amazement colored his words.

"I do indeed."

"Theodore had recently spent two years in South America." Encouraged by her reaction, he hastened to explain. "His work there has lent validity to the idea that one species had evolved from another due to adaptation to the environment. I saw a possibility in his research to believe that man, too, had evolved from other species, that he had not sprung full blown on this earth."

"You mean you questioned the story of Adam and Eve?" Douglas broke in, his words holding utter shock.

"It was perceived that I did, although I always told students that they had to decide for themselves...natural selection or Genesis or perhaps a mix of both. I never promoted either theory as correct. But locals went to the dean with the story that I had been teaching heresy. They also sent letters to the head of the church in York."

"How unfair," Lottie interjected.

"A furor erupted in the town." Jack shook his head. "I became the target of hatred. Worst of all, Cathy suffered not emotionally from the reaction of her friends but physically as well. She was injured in an attack against us...me in particular...one morning as we left the church."

"Oh, Jack, how awful! How could anyone be so cruel as to harm that lovely girl?"

"Shortly I received a letter from the church hierarchy informing me my position in Fredericton was at an end, and if I wished to continue in the church, I would have to take up work in a small community on the east coast, known as Riverhaven, with a population"—he glanced at Douglas—"of a number of dubious residents." He paused and spread out his hands. "And so here I am, a man branded a heretic, shamed within the church community even here. Now what do you say, Charlotte Dally? Will you still be willing to marry such a man?"

"Jack, I don't know. I have to think…"

"Bloody hell!" Douglas was on his feet and striding out of the room. "You're a pair of fools. I can see drastic measures are necessary."

Chapter Thirty-Six

Lottie was tidying up the schoolroom late one afternoon two weeks later. The children had been gone for some time before the door opened and Brodie MacMillan strode in with his usual swaggering strides. Behind him was his brother Douglas.

"Miss Lottie Danvers?" Brodie shocked her by addressing her by her former name. "I've been waitin' until you were sufficiently recovered to be up to bein' called a dashed fool before I was once again designated to play matchmaker in a difficult situation."

"Douglas, you told him!" The words were a gasp of consternation. "How could you!"

"I had to, Lottie. He's the only person on earth that I know can bring a happy conclusion to this mess."

"That I am." Brodie sat down on one of the benches used by the children. "Although I will admit, I'm gettin' a mite weary of playin' cupid to couples too dull to recognize they're meant to be together. If this continues, they'll be expectin' me to wear a diaper and carry a bow and quiver. Let me tell you, it will a cold day in hell when that happens."

"There will be no need for such drastic measures." Jack Wallace stepped out of Lottie's living quarters, a smile curling his lips. "Charlotte and I were married last evening, shortly after Reverend Edward Morgan and his family disembarked from the *Highland Lass*. It was a quiet ceremony, with the reverend's wife and daughter as witnesses and—"

"Bloody hell! So there was no need for me to get cleaned up in the middle of a workin' day, put on my best bib and tucker, and ride in here in the heat? Douglas"—he stood and punched his brother in the shoulder—"you might have gotten your facts straight before you gave me all this needless trouble."

"Brodie, I swear I had no idea." Douglas was quick to defend himself. "When I left them, it seemed as if they were still dawdling, prevaricating as they've been for weeks."

"Aw, well, it's all as we wished." Brodie held out a hand to Jack. "Congratulations, Jack." He turned to his brother. "Our work here may be done, but we've a deal more to get at. There has to be a party to celebrate these two. Best be on our way and get the ladies started on the cookin' for such. And I'll be tunin' my fiddle for the dancin'."

"Really?" Lottie held up an admonishing hand. "There's no need—"

"Aye, there is." Brodie swung back on her. "We have few enough occasions for celebrations in Riverhaven, and by God, you two won't deprive us of one. Come along, brother."

Brodie's arm about his brother's shoulders, the pair left the schoolhouse.

"I guess there'll be no stopping him." Grinning, Jack shrugged. "I've learned when Brodie MacMillan gets the bit in his teeth, it's safest to go along with him."

"Actually, I think it's a lovely idea." Lottie went to stand beside him and let him slip his arm about her shoulders. "We should proudly announce our marriage to the community...even if we won't be staying here."

"I hope you'll enjoy living in Fredericton, Charlotte. It might not always be easy. Not everyone will have forgiven me my studies or be willing to accept them, but at least I won't be accused of touting my views from the pulpit."

"I'll manage. I'm an adaptable woman, but are you sure you won't miss preaching?"

"Perhaps, but no matter what profession I'm in, I can still practice the golden rule as we've both done for a number of years. I will, however, miss Cathy."

"You can't prevent a young woman from falling in love." Lottie leaned against him, smiling. "And Geordie Fowler is a fine young man, with a solid future in the family business."

"Aye, of course."

"And when there are grandchildren, you and I will most definitely return to greet them."

"Grandchildren?" Shock registered in his voice and expression as he looked down at her.

"Of course, my love. We'll make wonderful grandparents...even if we're not all that old."

She took his hand and led him back into her living quarters and shut the door.

A word about the author...

Gail is the award-winning author of twenty-six published books. She is delighted to be an author with The Wild Rose Press, "where writers are encouraged, tutored and mentored in the best of ways," she says.

She makes her home in New Brunswick, the scene of many of her books, with her toller beagle.

Contact her at:

macgail@nbnet.nb.ca
Twitter: tollerbeagle44
Facebook: Gail MacMillan

CPSIA information can be obtained
at www.ICGtesting.com
Printed in the USA
LVHW080306140822
725894LV00027B/394

9 781509 240548